Praise for Merritt Tierce's

Love Me Back

"So ferocious, so powerful, so fearlessly told, that by the end I felt as though the wind had been knocked out of me. Even now I have the urge to walk down the street and give a copy to everyone I pass, pressing it into their hands, telling them, 'Read this. Read it now.' *Love Me Back* is that brilliant and that necessary." —Cristina Henríquez, author of *The Book of Unknown Americans*

"Hard to put down." —*The Dallas Morning News*

"One of my favorite books of the last few years."
—Carrie Brownstein, cocreator of *Portlandia*

"More or less tore my scalp off."
—Tom Nissley, *The Millions*

"Unforgettable."   —*Entertainment Weekly*

"Absolutely enthralling. . . . One of the most vital books about our invisible underclass I've read in years."
—Claire Vaye Watkins, author of *Battleborn*

Merritt Tierce

Love Me Back

Merritt Tierce, a National Book Foundation "5 Under 35" honoree, was born and raised in Texas. She received her MFA in fiction writing from the Iowa Writers' Workshop, where she was named a Meta Rosenberg Fellow, and she is a recipient of a Rona Jaffe Foundation Writers' Award. Merritt lives near Dallas with her husband and children.

www.merritttierce.com

Love
Me
Back

A Novel

Merritt Tierce

Anchor Books
A Division of Penguin Random House LLC
New York

FIRST ANCHOR BOOKS EDITION, JUNE 2015

Copyright © 2014 by Merritt Tierce

All rights reserved. Published in the United States by Anchor Books,
a division of Penguin Random House LLC, New York, and distributed in
Canada by Random House of Canada, a division of Penguin Random House
Ltd., Toronto. Originally published in hardcover by Doubleday, a division of
Penguin Random House LLC, New York, in 2014.

Anchor Books and colophon are registered trademarks of
Penguin Random House LLC.

Selected chapters were previously published, in slightly different form:
"Suck It" in *Southwest Review*, vol. 92, no. 3 (2007), and subsequently in *New
Stories from the South 2008: The Year's Best* edited by ZZ Packer (Chapel Hill:
Algonquin Books, 2008); "The Dangler" in *Reunion: The Dallas Review*, vol.
1 (2011); and "The Private Room" in *Dallas Noir*, edited by David Hale Smith
(New York: Akashic Books, 2013).

The Library of Congress has cataloged the Doubleday edition as follows:
Tierce, Merritt.
Love me back : a novel / Merritt Tierce.—First edition.
pages cm
1. Teenage mothers—Fiction.   2. Single mothers—Fiction.
3. Waitresses—Fiction.   4. Restaurants—Fiction.   I. Title.
PS3620.I365L68 2014
813.'6—dc23
2014003338

Anchor Books Trade Paperback ISBN: 978-0-345-80713-7
eBook ISBN: 978-0-385-53808-4

Book design by Maria Carella

www.anchorbooks.com

Printed in the United States of America
10 9 8 7 6 5 4 3 2

For Gretchen, who loved me forth,

and Evan, who loves me back.

Put Your Back into It

I met all four of them at an off-site catering event for the opening of their new Minimally Invasive Spine, Back, and Neck Group. The one I liked, Cornelius, was the only one I didn't sleep with, and the only one who asked me out. Trained at Yale so why was he asking out a waitress? I don't know. Two of the other three were sleazy and the handsomest was arrogant. One so sleazy I fled, though usually I had the stomach for it. Cornelius wore Tommy Bahama hibiscus-print silk shirts, and was more than twice my age, but who knows. Someone told him I was smart and gave him my number. We were to visit the Gordon Parks exhibit at the DMA on a Sunday afternoon. Gordon Parks was my idea and I knew it scored with him—maybe made him think of how I could be an accident, a good one lodged in the mire, just waiting to be sprung.

But late Saturday night I met my dealer in the parking lot of the Kroger on Cedar Springs and bought four twenties. At ten a.m. I hadn't come down even after smoking a joint and taking five sleeping pills. In the mirror I had no iris, I was all hole, falling in. I didn't answer when he called.

He'd asked me out the week before. It felt like a job interview but I went along. Would I be like Jordan? She was a young blond waitress liberated by one of her customers. Hedge fund. After they married they dined at The Restaurant often, before Stars or Mavs games. I'd never want to go back if I'd been her, I'd have felt afraid I might have dreamed it.

I didn't think that scenario likely, but still I would have answered if I'd been sober. When I recovered I left a message he didn't respond to. He'd given me one suspicious half-hearted bored chance and I turned out to be a flake. I never saw him in The Restaurant again. I can't believe he had that much pride.

The three others: I mentioned one so sleazy. Maybe in the end he wasn't as bad as the other two. I say that because he was uglier, and an ugly man may learn to compensate for his face with some kindness. Perhaps his entire career was compensation for his ugliness—a path to money that could pay women to ignore the way he looked. Pale pink, fat, he reminded me of a hairless mole we'd seen at the zoo. There is no point in asking what the attraction was—that's the wrong question. Clearly what has gone on in the world of my past can answer only other questions. Like why does a man want to pretend a woman likes him? What does anyone get from pretending? I did the ugly one first. Went to a bar in his neighborhood, drank some whiskey with him.

I ask my memory, Why did I take each next step? There was a hateful man who once said I am a step skipper but no, each step was taken. That one, then that one, then another, each *voluntary*. Whatever is in me that makes decisions is now full of an accretion of plaque, the chalky consequence of, paradoxically, so many hollow moments.

After the bar, his townhouse. One of those ubiquitous places that is nice and expensive but not special in any way. Three stories. On the first I took off my heels. On the second we reclined on a black leather couch and watched a giant television. He lay behind me and pushed his erection against me. I stared into no-space and regretted my life. On the third floor we got into his bed and he was so happy. He had done it. Gotten me there. Into the house, up the three stories, onto the bed. I couldn't not let him have it. I lay down next to him and turned my back to him and heard the drawer of the nightstand open. He hurried with the condom as if I might vanish. I let him penetrate me. No, I thought. No no no. I whispered it each time he pushed.

No.

No.

No. Hold on I have to pee, I said. I grabbed my purse from the dresser on the way into his bathroom. Marble floor, high ceiling, two steel sinks set into a long black counter-top. The coke looked sweet piled on the black counter and I could see my reflection above it. I looked worried. Don't worry, I said to myself, We're leaving.

I turned on both sinks. Surgeons don't do coke, they drink. I shaped two lines with my debit card and snorted them with a piece of a straw I kept in my purse. I licked the edge of the debit card. I licked the counter. I peed, and checked my nose in the mirror. I imagined her sitting on the counter, her short legs hanging off, swinging. I went back into the bedroom and said, I'm sorry, I have to go, I'm not well. I was shaking and I felt beautiful. I thought how beautiful it was that I had only one garment to put back on, my black cocktail dress there on the floor. I pulled it over my head. I don't wear underwear. See you, I said. He didn't try to stop me.

The other two go together. After work, after I'd served them their steaks at The Restaurant, I met them at a nightclub where we drank and danced. They'd come by cab but I had my car so when we left I drove. A tiny car, and they were both tall, they barely fit. The black one was at least six-five. The white one six-three maybe. The car spiraled around the parking garage of the apartment complex where the white one lived. Up and up and up to the top floor. I could tell they felt ridiculous in my car and it seemed like forever before I could park it. The black one was gorgeous and so composed. You knew he would get whatever he wanted in life. I stood between them and they undressed me. Isn't she pretty? the white one said. I loved that. How old is she? the black one asked. She's twenty-one, bro, it's cool, said the white one. I sucked on the white one while the black one fucked me. He came and then he lay down on the floor to sleep, he was too long for the white one's bed. I hated staying the night because it was always different in the morning. So when they were both passed out I left, back down the parking garage ramps. Down and down and down.

You'd work at The Restaurant every night and sometimes you'd see the same customers two or three times a week, and then sometimes you wouldn't see them for six months. The tall white spine surgeon disappeared for a while but then he came in with his family for Christmas and I took care of them. Good to see you, I said. You too, sweetie, how you been? he said. Someone told me—maybe it was the ugly one, unafraid to bash his own kind—that spine surgeons are weak among surgeons, that you can't really fix a back so you go in there and fuck around and bill the shit out of the insurance company and refer the patient to pain management.

The tall white one had a girlfriend or fiancée or something with him at that Christmas dinner. She was on his left and I stood on his right to tell the table about the features, which were presented in the raw and under plastic on a large rectangular ceramic platter I'd placed in the center of the table. I described in detail each cut displayed. At the end I said, This evening's market fish is a Chilean sea bass, pan-seared, and then I felt him reach between my legs and wrap his forearm around my shin, rub my calf. She couldn't see and neither could anyone else because my back was against a wall. Chef is serving the sea bass over grilled asparagus with a lump crab beurre blanc, I said.

I leaned forward to lift the platter off the table. I could sense another server standing behind me, waiting for it. It weighed twenty pounds so I had to brace myself by stepping forward with one foot and when I did the surgeon slid his hand up the inside of my thigh and put his thumb between my lips. He pressed hard, as if somehow I might not have felt any of it before that. I concentrated on my left hand as it raised the corner of the platter. I placed my right hand under the platter and concentrated on the marbling in the chateaubriand and on where the wineglasses underneath my elbows were. Oh that looks so heavy! exclaimed the girlfriend. It is, I said. Babe, help her, she said to the surgeon. She's got it, he said, since there was no subtle way he could extract his hand from between my legs just then. I'm fine, ma'am, I said, but if I throw my back out I've got your man's number. People tittered. I lifted the platter straight up and shelved it backward in space, knowing the server behind me would take it from me as soon as it cleared my guests' heads. I didn't turn around as DeMarcus said in my ear Thank you Mama and took the platter.

Let me know if you have any questions about the menu, I said to the table, and we'll be happy to accommodate any special requests. I looked at the older man across from me—probably the surgeon's father, who'd probably pay the check—and smiled.

Unless this one's asking, I said, gesturing at the spine surgeon by tipping the side of my head toward him while I sparkled at the older man. Then I looked down at the spine surgeon and said, I've got a big hot plate of nothing for you, sir.

He withdrew his hand and reached for his beer and they all laughed.

Part One

The Olive Garden

I'm a hard worker, I tell the manager. We are sitting in a booth. His name is Rajiv George and he is short and portly and has kind eyes. He laughs often. Great, he says. In a restaurant that's really all you need. We'll teach you everything else.

Does that mean I'm hired? I ask. The Olive Garden is the fourth restaurant to interview me. I filled out applications at thirteen.

I think so, he laughs. Congratulations. Are you sure you don't want a breadstick? He gestures at the basket of fluffy wands between us on the table. They glisten with garlic butter.

No thank you, I say. I ate earlier.

Well, you could use some meat on your bones. He twinkles so I try to twinkle back. Employees can have as much bread and soda as they want, he says.

Okay, I say. When do I start?

Now? he asks. It's only three thirty. You can learn how to make salads and help out tonight. The salad girl called in sick. Word to the wise, if you're gonna call in, do it as early as possible. Actually—the wise don't call in. Find someone to cover the shift. Right, Kendall? He says this to a tall, stunning man who walks past the booth, then pauses to tie on a black apron with three pockets across the front. His white shirt is unbuttoned and I see a leather necklace with a pewter cross that hangs so it just touches the beginning of his chest fur, visible over the top edge of a wife-beater. His sleeves are rolled up and he has snakes tattooed around both forearms.

Right, boss, he says. Who's this?

He is facing Mr. George, but means me. He pops up his collar and buttons the top button, then takes a blue tie out of one of his apron pockets and ties it with quick aggressive movements. There is a grease spot he is careful to hide within the knot.

This is Marie, says Mr. George. She's new.

No shit, says Kendall. How old is she? Twelve?

Excuse him, says Mr. George. He was in Desert Storm.

I was in fourth grade during Desert Storm but I don't say this. I won a lot of mental math competitions that year including the regional title and I didn't pay attention to the news. But we had to write letters to the soldiers, and the math team coach made us tie yellow ribbons on our competition pencils. Kendall extends his right hand to me while rolling down the sleeve with his left.

Christopher Kendall, he says. Marie, I say, shaking his hand. It is warm and dry and strong. He has a silver Celtic knot ring on his thumb.

You ain't got a last name, Cabbage Patch?

Cut it out, Mr. George says to Christopher. I just hired

her, don't run her off yet. At least not before she fills in for the salad girl tonight.

Young, I say to Christopher. Yes you are, he says. Did you give her the tour? he asks Mr. George.

No, says Mr. George. Are you volunteering? Don't think it gets you out of opening sidework.

Why do you think I want a little helper? says Christopher, and to me, Come on, doll, I'll show you around.

Don't forget what we talked about last night, says Mr. George as we walk away from the booth toward the swing door that leads into the kitchen.

Fuck your mother, Apu, Christopher says under his breath. Raj is harmless, he says to me. But don't eat the bread or you'll wind up like him and that would be tragic. He gives me a blatant up-and-down as he says tragic.

This is the back station, he says. We are standing in front of a soda machine and a computer screen. He continues, By the bar is the front station. Over in the twenties is the side station. Back station is safest. Ring at the bar and somebody's gonna ask you for change, or when the dingbat hostess leaves the door you'll end up seating. Side station is right between two big-tops so somebody is bound to need something, and there's always a fucking kid throwing crayons on the floor. Parents think you're a prick if you don't stop everything and pick em up for Johnny. Nobody can see you here.

Okay, I say. He takes a clear plastic cup from a stack by the soda machine and plunges it into the ice. Plastic for us, glass for them, he says. Always use the ice scoop. Georgie sees you doing this you'll get yelled at. It's unsanitary. Plus if you break a glass in the ice we have to burn it. Where is the ice scoop? I ask. Fuck if I know, he says. He fills his cup with Mountain Dew and takes a straw wrapped in paper from a cardboard box on the stainless-steel shelf above the soda machine. He tears the paper about an inch from the top of the straw, throwing away the long part and leaving the short part on like a cap. He stabs the straw into the cup. This is how you serve a soda, he says. Make sure it's full. Fuckers drink it like it's fucking crack. Put a straw in it. Leave the top on the straw so they know you didn't put your nasty paws all over where their mouth goes. Always have extra straws in your apron because some lazy asshole in the section next to you won't give his people straws, and when you walk by they'll ask you for one, and if you don't have one you gotta find dipshit or get it yourself. He takes the paper cap off the straw and flicks it into the trash. The fizzing head on the soda has settled so he tops it off and then takes a big suck. I recommend a straw for your personal consumption as well, he says. Never put your mouth on anything in a restaurant if you can help it. Shit doesn't get clean. Ever.

Okay, I say. Yo, is that all you say? he asks.

No, I say, but I'm here to work. He raises his eyebrows at this and says, Oh! He looks around. She's here to work, he says to another server who walks by with a gray plastic tub of silverware. Great, says the other server, I need help with these rollups.

Sorry, Dave, I called her first, says Christopher. This way, honey.

He takes my elbow and guides me toward the kitchen.

Dave's a faggot, but he's a good guy, he says. I heard that, says Dave.

Outside the kitchen door hangs a broom and dustpan. There's the broom, says Christopher. Somebody breaks a glass use it. Don't pick it up with your hands. Tell one of the busboys you're busy and make them do it.

He kicks open the kitchen door and points up at a circular mirror hanging from the ceiling. Coming out, check that or you'll knock somebody down and then people will think you're stupid. Going in, look through the window. First time you bump a tray out of somebody's hands is not gonna be pleasant for you, or them, and if it's me you're doing all my sidework for a week. Trays, tray jacks, he says, gesturing toward a stack of big brown ovals and wooden stands with black nylon straps. You can carry a tray, right?

I don't know, I say. He gives me his full attention for the first time. Wait, he says. You ever worked in a restaurant before?

No, I say. I fucking knew it, he says, I could tell the second I saw you. He shakes his head slowly, looking around the kitchen. A skinny boy in a white coat is chopping onions. He looks up at us. A tear slides down his nose and he raises his shoulder to rub it off. Don't cry, José, don't cry, says Christopher. José says I'm sorry, Chris, it's just so sad how ugly your mom is, but Christopher doesn't answer because another server comes into the kitchen through the door at the opposite end. Sup Chris, says the new server, then Sup Kelly, Tare-Bear to two women who are standing in a corner talking while they do their makeup. Hey Josh, says Christopher, guess what we got here. Josh is punching in on the time clock by the office. Mr. George sticks his head out and says Don't punch in unless you're working. I'm working, I'm working, says Josh. What do we got, Chris?

A fucking virgin, everybody. Chris grabs my hand and yanks it up into the air like I won a boxing match. This is Marie, and today's her first day in a restaurant. Welcome to hell, baby. He laughs a sadistic laugh. He has beautiful beautiful teeth. I pull my hand down and look toward the office but Mr. George is on the phone, his back to us.

Don't look at him, says Christopher. You gotta make it with us. He don't know shit about how to wait tables.

I nod. I know, I say, I was just looking at the clock.

Uh-huh, says Christopher. There's only two times in a restaurant: before and after. You walk in, you white-knuckle it, try not to fuck up till it's over and then it's over. You made money or you didn't.

God, leave her alone, Chris, says one of the women. Ignore him, she says to me. He's so full of himself it's disgusting.

Christopher walks toward her so I follow him. What's disgusting, Tara, he says softly, is how full of me *you'd* like to be. Fuck off, says Kelly. Tara yells toward the office, Raj, Chris is harassing me again! but then both women start giggling. Don't worry, sweetie, Kelly says. He's all talk. That's not what she said last night, says Christopher. Kelly rolls her eyes. Fine, you win, she says. I would rather fuck myself with an OG bread stick but you can pretend if you want.

Don't believe anything he says, she tells me as she pushes

open the kitchen door with her back, pulling her hair up into a ponytail.

How old are you, anyway, asks Christopher, leading us into a humid room off the kitchen where a man in a plastic apron says Hola. He is using a big nozzle on a spring to spray some large metal pans in a deep sink. This is the dish pit, yells Christopher over the noise of the water and the clanking of the pans. And watch out, they haven't put down the mats yet. You got good shoes? He leans over and pinches my pant leg away from my knee, lifting the hem so he can see my black canvas sneakers. He has three fingers behind my knee, and when he closes his hand his thumb is so high up on my inseam I look at him to see what it means. He looks at me back and squeezes as he says Those won't work. You need some nonslip soles or you'll wind up on your ass wearing cannelloni. Payless in the mall has some cheap ones.

I'll be eighteen in two weeks, I say, adding a year. He whistles. He puts an arm around my shoulder and yells at the dishwasher, pointing at me with his other hand, Hey José, es una bambina!

Stop, I say. What? he says. I just said you're a babe. I know what you said, I say. Ella hablas español también, he yells at José. No me llamo José, says the dishwasher. He sticks out a wet red hand. Mario, he says. Marie, I say, shaking his hand. Ah, Maria! he says. Somos gemelos! I smile. Mucho gusto, I say. Come on, says Christopher, enough fucking around. Let's get to work.

———

The third man I'd ever had sex with was an ex–corrections officer who is six-four and the most gorgeous man I've ever seen or ever will. It may seem rash to hand out that superlative to someone I met as a teenager, but perfection cannot be perfected. His teeth were perfectly square, even, and white, his smile dazzling beneath thick blue-black hair, his eyes a brilliant unseen color of bottle green backlit with navy, his olive skin so smooth and taut it made you feel that if you closed your eyes you might be his, you might be somewhere else. In the restaurant where we worked, he would take four crates of clean glasses from the dish machine, stack them, and balance them above his shoulder with one arm to bring them into the kitchen. I could barely lift two to chest level using my whole body. But there was no bulk, he was just on the solid side of lean. The strength in him was panther-dark and menacing and in spite of the ordinary green lines across the toes of his dress socks I was too scared of him to get wet. He fucked me anyway, with a giant penis I couldn't bring myself to look at. I was like a child, I was quiet and tense and bit my tongue and lip to keep silent when he pulled out and ground himself to a sterile stop on me. Pushing through every layer of sensitive tissue and fat to pin me to the bed, he succeeded in giving himself an orgasm, avoiding ejaculation, controlling his breathing, and keeping his face composed. He made no sound and took no notice of me—I knew of his completion only through the ripples against my mons. Later when I put my hand on his on the gearshift on the way back to the restaurant he said from behind his aviators Do you know what the words *No one* mean. Three weeks later he was fired in the middle of a shift for harassing the underage salad girl and I had to take over his tables.

———

I think he could tell I was pregnant the day we did it. I don't think he cared. I begged him to fuck me. I followed him around the restaurant, touching him. I stood next to him when we sang Buona Festa. I didn't even know how to fuck. It was four months then but I still didn't show through my clothes at five, or six and a half. At seven I had to move the apron down to my hips. I worked there until she was born.

———

We went back to the restaurant together that day because we were both between doubles. I know that's what we did but I forget that. It seems like I stayed on the bed and he left. I see myself naked. I hadn't touched my belly yet. I never looked at it. Christopher didn't answer my phone calls. I started calling him that night after work but he never answered. I called him all the time. I knew he wouldn't answer but then I would be calling him without even knowing why or what I would say. In the restaurant he'd say Hey if I said Hey Christopher but he never said my name and he ignored me. I see myself on the bed naked calling him. Christopher. Christopher. If he would just answer I would touch my belly.

———

I never wore makeup in high school so I didn't know how to do it. But I bought some Maybelline at the drugstore and I spread it on my face. It made me look older and ugly. Even though he ignored me I would wait in the parking lot until I saw his Camaro pull in and then I would time my walk so we reached the employee entrance at the same time. The day I wore the makeup I couldn't tell he was looking at me because of the sunglasses but he said Come here when we got close to the door. What is it, I said. I was standing next to him and he had his hand on the door but he took it away from the handle and pulled me to him by my arm. I tripped forward and he shoved me back. I just need to get this shit off your chin, he said. Jesus. He rubbed across my jawline with the heel of his fist and then took a handkerchief out of his pocket and wiped his hand on it. He whipped the hand-kerchief unfolded with a snap and pressed it to my face with his palm. I was humiliated but his hand was on my face and that was the first time he had touched me since that other afternoon. I could feel the warmth of his hand on my whole face and I could smell his aftershave and I put my hand up over his hand, to push his hand into my face harder. He jerked his hand down when I did that. What are you doing you little freak, he said. Go wash your face.

I washed my face in the women's restroom. We weren't supposed to use the front-of-house restrooms even before the restaurant was open. I hadn't broken any rules before that but I didn't want to use the employee restroom because it was unisex and anyone who came in would see me. When I came out of the restroom there was the pay phone between the women's and the men's restrooms and I picked up the receiver and called the baby's father. We weren't supposed to use the phone ever. My ear was still wet from washing my face. I called him collect. He answered on the first ring and the operator said Will you accept the charges from Marie Young and he said Yes and then he said Are you okay? and I said Let's get married.

———

I tried to stiff my busser once. I didn't know anything. I hadn't made any money that night. Maybe thirty-five dollars and it was two days past my due date. We were supposed to give the busser three percent of our sales and they had to initial the cashout. I just skipped that part and the busser said something to Tara. She confronted me and said Mama I know you're about to pop and all but that shit is not cool. Give him his money and don't ever do that again. He's got a family too.

I'm so sorry, I said to him. I know he was mad when he told Tara but when I told him I was sorry he hugged me and said it was okay. I gave him the money. It was only six dollars.

My mother thought I was trying to lose you. The midwife told me if I didn't start gaining weight she was going to put me in the hospital. I weighed one hundred twenty-eight pounds when I got pregnant with you, and at the end of the first three months I weighed one hundred ten. I woke up sick, in the same bedroom I'd been sleeping in since I was four. I'd puke at six in the morning and lie on the floor in the bathroom in my robe with the shower running on cold so there'd still be hot water when I could finally stand. I listened to the running water and took tentative mouse-bites of a banana. I was a temp at the corporate office of Sally Beauty Company and I would puke there at nine. The restrooms were too far from my cubicle, so every day I puked in my trash can.

I was supposed to be compiling the departments' Y2K contingency plans into a comprehensive binder for my boss but instead I read *The Seven Storey Mountain*. My boss wanted everything in binders so if I heard someone coming toward my cubicle I popped open the binder rings and then snapped them shut. I usually puked again around noon. Sometimes I made it until two. After the third puke I would be painfully hungry. Shaky, dizzy, pale. I would eat my lunch slowly over the last two hours of the workday but on the drive home I would puke one more time.

At night I would call your dad, who was working as a trim carpenter for his uncle's contracting business in East Texas. He spent the day wiping sweat out of his eyes so he wouldn't miss with the nail gun or the circular saw, finishing closets and chair rail and laying baseboard and trying not to keel over from heatstroke. We talked about how we'd never want to live in that kind of house, the two-car garage most of what you saw from the street. As if a house was mainly a place to keep your cars. We talked about that but not as if we assumed we would live together in a house. Not as a joint assertion of what we wanted for our unified future. Or maybe he did mean it that way but he knew I didn't.

I didn't want to talk about Sally so I asked questions about housebuilding while the pauses between my questions and his answers got longer and longer and finally he'd say Well I'm passing out, I guess I'll let you go, I have to get up early. And I'd say Don't let me go and he'd say quietly We'll figure it out, Marie, but we never talked about it. It felt like if one of us would make a decision the other would accept it, but neither of us knew how to take the lead.

We had spent only five days together. Spring break of our senior year, 1999, but I had skipped a grade so I was sixteen and he was eighteen. We met on a mission trip to Mexico. We were next to each other on the airplane and it was like we had always known each other. In our ordinary environments I would have thought he was too popular and good-looking for me and he would have thought I was too smart for him, but we had none of that context to impede us, and as the plane circled down over the vast bowl of Mexico City he leaned across me to look out the window, letting his arm press against mine. That was so much then. Look, I said, it goes on forever. The colorful jumbled squares of buildings spread out in all directions. When it was our turn to exit the plane he stepped into the aisle and motioned for me to go in front of him. I reached overhead for my backpack but he was a head taller and said I got it, Shorty.

They told me the sickness would stop at twelve weeks but it didn't. The temp position at Sally wasn't renewed, probably because the CPA stationed next to me was tired of listening to me puke. At fifteen weeks I woke up at six and went into the bathroom and knelt by the commode, but then I realized I didn't need to puke, and the strange new fluttering in my belly was you.

Chili's

It looked like you were selling drugs to Barrett, says Kevin. Kevin is the general manager of the Chili's where I work. He is attractive but has a sour edge. So I can't let you keep working here, he says.

I have a bad habit of becoming quieter and quieter the more important it is that I say something. I stare at Kevin's shoes. I did sell Barrett the drugs. About thirty Vicodins left over from wisdom teeth. But I don't use drugs. I don't even drink. I am thinking about whether or not it is ironic that I am being fired for selling drugs when I know I am much less advanced in the field than my coworkers. That Alanis Morissette song about isn't it ironic is always playing on the sound system and I overheard one of my tables talking about how nothing in the song was actually ironic. I wanted to say Isn't that ironic? but the people are not there for you. They are there for the food and the people they came with.

I am so clueless I brought the pills to work in the prescription bottle, and then poured them into a plastic ramekin in the to-go station by the back door. Kevin walked by right as Barrett handed me some money and I handed him some pills. I went about my sidework and I suppose Kevin went about thinking over what he'd seen because he didn't call me into the office until the shift was over.

Even though I haven't said anything Kevin waffles. I don't get it, he says. I know you have a baby. You're a hard worker. I saw Damon has you closing three times this week.

I like closing, I say. Well I can't have people selling drugs in the restaurant, he says. I know, I say. Kevin says I mean, it's one thing if Barrett had a headache or something and you gave him some medicine you had. And then he happened to owe you some money for some reason. Is that what happened?

Yes, I say emphatically, finally looking up at him. After a long pause Kevin says Okay. Go finish your station. If Barrett has a headache we have Advil in the first-aid kit.

I'm sorry, I say. Thank you.

Barrett had emo hair and ear gauges and wore one of those black belts with all the silver metal studs. He had mesmerizing eyes, the rare and exact shade of the pale flesh of a honeydew melon; unfortunately for his habits his eyes were sensitive, the irises nearly translucent and the whites prone to red. He kept Visine in his apron and I'd see him putting the drops in all the time but always in a walk-in or dry storage or somewhere the managers didn't usually go. He slouched around in his slip-on Vans and had only one mild speed. You can't be in the weeds if you don't care, he said.

———

At night she slept with us and when he got up at five to take a shower she stirred. I put her in her car seat and set it on the floor in the bathroom while he showered. She'd fall right to sleep again in there, I guess because the sound of the water and the steam were nice. I went back to bed and he left for the job site at five forty and she slept in the bathroom until seven thirty, when she got hungry and cried. I went to get her and her diaper was heavy and she fussed while I changed it but then I lay back down with her and nursed her and we both fell asleep again until nine or so. This was what we did every morning. Then laundry or some other house-work. She was a calm quiet baby. She was happy. And if she cried I nursed her and she was fine again.

———

That was the best body I ever had, and the worst mind. I was seventeen. I was slender and strong and I also had swol-len C-cup breasts. I had never even worn a bra before my milk came in for her, and I had always been ashamed of my breasts before then. The way they looked if I leaned over. Sad little triangular flaps of skin just holding my nipples to my chest. If I was lying on my back they disappeared com-pletely and I could have been a boy except that my nipples were big and square. I had no breast tissue. I didn't feel like a girl when I was a child. I didn't feel female. I felt neutral. Then I had her and I had breasts and I felt like I had become a girl. Femininity is shocking. Women always seem smaller and softer than I expect, when I hug them. Even if they don't look small or soft. When I had breasts I was aware of them all the time. They were something new in my field of vision and they made my body intrude into another plane of space. But my mind was an open sore. It was black. I couldn't tell if I was deep inside it or totally outside it. I would imagine being fatally cleaved all day long. By a gallows axe, the T-shaped kind. By a heavy medieval sword like Excalibur. Or bludgeoned, usually blows to my head, usually by the butt of a rifle.

I don't know what we did all day. I went for walks with her. I read while she nursed. Magazines and biographies mostly. I would go to the library and take one of the subscription cards from something that looked interesting and check Bill Me and then I would get two or sometimes three issues before they cut it off. I used to read the magazines at the library, because there was a nice overstuffed chair there and I could put my leg up to support her while she nursed, which was the most comfortable position. If she was nursing on the left I would put my left leg up with my knee bent and my foot in the chair and that way I didn't have to put all her weight on my arm. Then I would switch. Then she would fall asleep. I could read through three or four magazines that way. But one day when it was exceptionally quiet there she was smacking and swallowing and I liked the sound myself but it's not a subtle sound. There's no mistaking it. I didn't mess with any of those awkward cloths they sell to cover you while you nurse, I just lifted my shirt and put her on. But we were good at it, you would never see my nipple or even my skin the way we did it. Still the reference librarian came up to me that one day and she stopped about five feet away from the chair like I was contagious and she leaned toward me and whispered I'm sorry honey but you can't do that here. About that time the baby choked because the milk was flowing so hard and she came off the nipple and the streams were pulsing out into the air. The milk went all over my shirt and the baby's face. She started crying and I had to put my hand right on my breast and push on it because that was the only thing that would stop it. I said Okay to the librarian and I stood up with the baby but I knew she wouldn't stop crying until I put her back on, so I turned away from the librarian and got her nursing again while I was standing there. Then I said Would you mind putting these magazines back for me. We walked out. There was nobody there.

At home we slept some more. I was always that heavy, iron kind of tired. My exhaustion was metallic. Sharp, flat, invincible. And I was always hungry because she was always hungry. For my shift meal I would have the black-bean burger plain with Swiss and I would eat every bite and every French fry and I would drink the chocolate milk shake with the sprinkles every night. And I still couldn't sit on the floor or in a wooden chair because there was nothing to support my bones. Even if the floor was carpet I was so thin it hurt. I ate whatever I wanted and it all turned into milk.

When he got home at four thirty in the afternoon I would be dressed for work and finishing nursing her one last time. She was six months old when I started there so while I was at work he would give her some mashed banana or some rice cereal and sometimes a bottle of water. By the time I got home at eleven or midnight my breasts would be huge rocks and I would get into bed and wake her up and nurse her for a long time, both sides. That always felt so good, when they were that full and I could finally nurse her. I had to be careful at work the last hour or so because if I thought of her or heard a baby cry sometimes I would feel the pricking of the milk letting down and I would have to try to push on my breasts without anyone seeing, but most of the time when you're waiting tables you're doing something with your hands or you're in front of people. Once or twice I couldn't stop it because I was taking an order or running food and the milk soaked through my shirt. When it happened the first time I was wearing a blue shirt and two dark round circles appeared on my chest. We could wear blue, red, or black Chili's shirts, polos with the embroidered red pepper logo. After that I always wore the black shirt.

———

I never called or visited my parents, after we got our own place. They didn't live far from us but I didn't know what to report. I hate that I hate my life? They were there when she was born and they were insatiable for her but I didn't feel like she was my baby while we lived with them. They were always taking her from me. Now I realize that was nothing more than the ravenous craving of a grandparent for the bodily wonder—the heft, the face, the smell—of a grandchild. At the time I was afraid that everyone could tell how lost I was, how lacking in maternal instinct, how sad. At the time I thought they thought I wasn't fit to have her, but I was afraid to call them on it and hear them say what I thought was true. So I let them take her from me and give her back to me when she was hungry, as if I were only her nursemaid.

Home was the one place I nursed her in private, so no one could watch me try to be her mother.

When she was three months old I found an apartment for the three of us and we moved out. I let my husband explain it to them because they couldn't talk to him the way they talked to me, and I didn't know what to say. My mother said You don't have to do this as she handed me the baby. I didn't respond. I just took the baby and started fitting her into her car seat. My husband said to my mother, who had started to cry, Hey. It'll be fine. I'll take care of her. We're just across town.

———

My dad came up to the Chili's one night to check on me. My husband had probably told them I wasn't doing well. He talked to them more than I did but it wasn't a conspiracy. I didn't talk to anyone and he liked people so he did. My dad ate a Paradise Pie while I waited for the last table on the other side of the restaurant to leave so I could finish the closing duties. I was sweeping my station, pulling out the empty booths to pick up menus and crayons that had fallen in the cracks. He sat in a booth and talked to me while I swept. I think he was trying to convince me to hang in there. I listened but I knew I wouldn't. I learned a lot of things while I worked there. I learned how to sweep aggressively and efficiently. I learned how to anticipate and consolidate, which is all waiting tables is. I learned how to use work to forget. I learned how to have an orgasm and I learned I was a bad wife.

I didn't have the constant decapitating images at work. At work my mind became gray and busy and it was okay. But the next morning I would see a butcher knife plunged into my chest, pinning me to the bed. Or a machete that would go through my pelvis and all the way through the mattress and the box spring to the floor below.

Eating scrambled eggs or toast in the kitchen I was afraid for her. I cried and moved slowly all day long. I thought it must be bad for her to have that as her mother. So far away. She was like her dad. The same peachy complexion and disposition, the same red hair, the same feet.

I didn't talk to her. I was a silent mother. Touching was talking. I smelled her a lot, especially her breath, which smelled like butter.

———

I don't remember much about working there. I remember the to-go girl was incredibly good at her job and that was the first time I had ever seen anyone work smart and hard like that. The phone on her shoulder, the competent look on her face, how she shaved a fraction of a second off her process by not letting the cash drawer open all the way. The tough way she stapled the order chit to the bag. I wanted to be like her and not like Barrett. It wasn't that I liked waiting tables so much then—it was that I had somewhere to be. Some function in life. I didn't understand how to be a wife or mother. But there were rules to being a waitress. The main one was don't fuck up. Another was whatever you skip in your prep will be the one thing you need when you're buried. If you look at the stack of kids' cups while you're tying

on your apron in the afternoon and decide there will probably be enough for the night because you really don't want
to go out to the shed and dig around for the new sleeve, eight
soccer teams will come in at nine, and you'll have to go out
to the shed anyway, and by the time you get back you'll have
killed your tips on all your other tables. That incessant ful-
fillment of Murphy's Law taught me to be superstitious. I
never said It looks like it's going to be a slow night and we'll
get out early because that would suddenly make the smoking
section fill up. The smokers took forever. You could never
turn those tables because they just weren't in a hurry. They
smoked before they ordered. They always had appetizers
and drinks. They smoked after the appetizers. They always
had dessert. Their tabs were inevitably more, but they undid
it by staying there for so long you could have had three $25
tables instead of one $40, even though the smokers tipped
better. And I never said I think we're going to be busy tonight
because then it would be dead and they wouldn't cut anyone
and you'd stand around for six $2.13 hours. If I knocked
over a saltshaker while I was refilling it or wiping down a
table I always threw a pinch over my left shoulder.

———

I got chlamydia from John Smith. That was actually his
name. John Fucking Smith, said my husband. You cheated
on me with John Fucking Smith?

Yes, I said. Do you have to call it cheating?

What the fuck does it matter what I call it, Marie. Is
there anyone else? he said.

Yes, I said.

What? he said. His eyes went hard then and he crossed his arms. We were standing in the ugly galley kitchen of our apartment. It was right next to a highway. It never got dark at night and I pretended the constant sound of the traffic was the ocean. It was an all bills paid one-bedroom and the rent was $397. We stood in the kitchen under the fluorescent lights. His face was so white and his eyes were so black. He was still and I heard a semi downshift and I could hear the lightbulbs buzzing and a moth flicking around inside the fixture. Then he lunged away from the counter and I covered my head even though he was the most gentle person I'd ever known. He started kicking the oven. Kicking kicking kicking. Stop! I yelled. Stop! The baby cried from our bed.

He stopped kicking the oven. Did you even make it a year? Tell me, he said.

Yes, I said.

Chlamydia, he said. Fuck you, Marie, he said. The baby was crying louder. He took his keys off the counter and went to the door. He put on one boot and lost his balance while he was putting on the other and dropped his keys and then he said Fuck fuck fuck fuck fuck! and jammed his foot into the boot and stood up and punched the wall next to the door. It made a hole in the sheetrock and he bent over and held his hand between his legs. He picked up his keys and slammed the door behind him. The baby was crying so hard she was losing her breath between screams. I went into our bedroom to get her and the neighbor above us stomped on the ceiling and shouted Shut up, man!

I lay down on the bed with the baby and shushed her. She smelled so sweet and she was so soft and warm. She made the most urgent little sounds as she latched on to my nipple. Shh, I said. She stopped crying and nursed until she fell asleep again.

———

Business had been so sluggish the night before Thanksgiving that Damon, the assistant manager, cut down to just me by eight thirty, and I walked out with $32, twenty of which was given to me by a man who had a cup of tortilla soup and a Shiner and said he was sorry I had to work the night before a holiday. When I got out I went to the Albertsons next door and bought bananas, brown rice, black beans, a yellow onion, a can of Ro*Tel, and everything to bake a pumpkin pie. I never baked so I didn't have any of the spices or sugar or flour at home, or a pie pan. I had eight dollars left after checking out so I stopped for gas on the way home.

The next day I made the pie using the recipe on the back of the can. We were still getting WIC cereal and milk so breakfast was Kix and bananas. Thanksgiving dinner was the rice and beans with the onion and Ro*Tel added for flavor, which is what we usually ate, and the pie. He said the pie was the best thing he had ever eaten in his life. I let the baby eat some of the filling off my fingers and she went nuts for it too, flapping her short baby arms. Then we all fell asleep at about five and he got up to pee a couple hours later. When he came back he said For some reason it hurts when I piss. I said Really? but I didn't say anything else, even though I knew that I had given Damon chlamydia and I knew I'd slept with my husband since then. Damon said it felt like he was pissing glass, and when he went to his doctor they stuck a Q-tip up his dick and he said it made him cry it hurt so bad. I went to the health department because we didn't have health insurance. They said I did have it, even though I didn't have symptoms. They gave me the medication to get rid of it. Damon asked me who else I'd been with because there was no way he'd given it to me. I said John and Luke and he said John gave it to you. I didn't ask how he knew but I knew he was right. Luke had just broken up with a girlfriend he'd been with for six years and he'd told me he had never cheated on her. I had to tell John and Luke and I never saw them except at work so I had to tell them at work. John didn't act surprised. That again, he said. Luke said You're kidding and then he said I knew it was a bad idea. A few days after that there was an awkward moment when Damon was voiding something for John at a computer screen and Luke and I walked up at the same time to ring. I had told John about Damon and Luke but I hadn't told Luke about the other two because I knew he would have cared. Damon caught my eye and fumbled his manager card. I could feel Luke looking at me so I walked away like I had forgotten something.

I had thought about telling my husband but I kept putting it off. The day I decided I had to tell him I went to the apartment complex's laundry center to wash a load of whites. His undershirts, the baby's burp cloths and diapers and onesies, and our bath towels and dishrags. Our apartment was right across the parking lot from the laundry center so I started the washer and then checked on the baby who was asleep in her swing. I took a book outside and sat on the stairs in front of our door but I couldn't read. I watched ants carry off pieces of a Cheeto. Half an hour later I went to put the clothes in the dryer and the laundry room smelled awful, like shit. I opened the lid of the washer to take out our clothes and there was shit all over the stuff at the top. The smell made me gag and I let the lid fall and backed away from the washer. I didn't know what it meant but I didn't want to touch the clothes. On my way out the door I had to walk past a wooden bench and there was a foot-long turd on it. Only a human could have made it. When my husband got home I told him someone had wiped their ass with our laundry. He couldn't believe it either so he went to look. We left all our things in the washer because I said I wasn't going to let any of it touch the baby even if we washed it again and he agreed. But then I didn't want to tell him about the chlamydia.

———

I did make it one year exactly. I first fucked John the day after our anniversary. I have a picture of the three of us at the Macaroni Grill. We went there because it was another Brinker concept so I could use my employee discount. Neither of us was old enough to drink. We ordered virgin daiquiris and played hangman and tic-tac-toe on the paper tablecloth. Roses are red, he wrote with the red crayon. Violets are blue, I wrote with the blue. What do you want? he wrote. I didn't finish it because our food arrived. Our waitress took the picture. You guys are so cute, she said. He's holding the baby and has one arm around me and we're both smiling for real because the baby is grabbing his beard.

The next night I went to a park with John after work.

There was a jogging path that went back into some woods and we walked down it until we came to a bench. We sat down and it was so dark. He put his arm around me and brushed my nipple with his fingertips but I said Wait because I knew it would make me lactate and then we made out and I felt the milk, warm and soaking into the cloth circles I wore inside my bra. He tasted like onions but he was a good kisser. He had a nice face. Gray eyes with long eyelashes and dimples when he smiled. Soft spiky black hair. He pulled me into his lap and kissed my neck and said So you want this. Yes, I said. I waited for you in the walk-in. He paused and looked at me. No one falls for that, he said.

He grew up on the streets of St. Louis, he said. He told me he never knew his dad and he was taken from his mother and put in foster care when he was seven. He smelled like amber, wood, musk, earth. He exuded sex but at no one in particular. He talked to you while he chewed and bits of lettuce fell out of his mouth, then he belched, then he offered to refill your water. If he came up behind me at a computer terminal sometimes he would stand close enough to me so I could feel his erection and once he said Meet me in the walk-in.

Come on then, he said, and stood up holding me. I put my feet on the ground and unzipped his pants. He unzipped mine and turned me around so I was facing the bench. He pulled down my pants and I knelt on the bench, bracing myself against the back of it. It wasn't very comfortable and I had bruises on my knees the next day.

On his chest the tattooed face of a pit bull he said was the best friend he'd ever had, on his left calf a beckoning, bare-titted mermaid. Over his entire back a flaming skull, the fire burning up toward the nape of his neck and the jaw narrowing to a chin cleft at his tailbone. On his wedding finger a black band where a ring would go, on his left upper arm a cross made of scar tissue that stretched from shoulder to elbow, which he cut in with a knife in his other hand. Uncircumcised and he'd once had a Prince Albert but said it stopped him from penetrating as hard as he wanted to.

———

September was John, October was Luke, and November was Damon. There was some overlap which is how they all got the disease but John was unreliable and Luke felt bad about it and Damon was into me so he's the one I started seeing regularly. John lived in a shitty efficiency and I went over there sometimes if he said I could stop by and sometimes I went without asking. Most of the time he wasn't there, even when he'd said I could come over. He had a twin mattress on the floor of the apartment but he'd put it up in front of the bathroom when I was there and we did it on the carpet. I think he didn't want me to get the idea that he wanted me. I remember one time he told me I looked good and one time I told him his bread was moldy.

Luke was the one I should have wanted. He was tall and too good-looking. He had a deep voice that made me wish for so many things and he had a pretty bird dog. I've never liked dogs but that one was fine. Eric. He was a lot like Luke. Calm and well-bred. Luke told me how they'd go for a run and Eric would suddenly flash into a bush and Luke would find him rigid, stuck in his pointer pose, staring at some prey concealed in the brush. Luke would have to pick him up and set him down somewhere else before he would release his muscles. One afternoon we were all three on Luke's bed and Luke was lying behind me. He started rubbing my ass over and over, soft and unhurried. Petting me. I felt so contained. He was always so warm, like he had a fever. When he had rubbed my ass through my jeans for a long time he nudged me up on my knees in front of him and unbuttoned his jeans with one hand while he breathed in my ear and put his other hand up my shirt. He found my nipple and slid his thumb across it and back across it. Then he moved his hand down to my pants and unbuttoned them and pushed them down. He put his penis against my lips. I never got very wet for anyone but for him that day I was slick and he took so long to ease himself inside me. So slow. I had my head down on the bed by Eric because there was nowhere else to put it and I had a hand on his flank. He smelled clean and he was just lying there watching us. Luke pressed into me so slow that by the time he was all the way in I was massaging Eric's flank with one hand and his shoulder with the other. Mashing on him like a cat making biscuits. I didn't really know I was doing it but I had to put the intensity somewhere. I could feel Luke getting harder and longer and then he reached over me and pushed Eric off the bed. He took hold of one of my wrists and gathered the other wrist up in his grip so he was pulling my arms tight away from my head and pressing my wrists down into the bed. I was so much shorter than he was that he still had his other hand on the small of my back. Pushing it down firm on his cock. He held me in place like that and I kept myself taut against him almost as if I were trying to resist or get away but it was the best thing I had ever felt with a man.

———

Damon had smooth knotty forearms. I'd never been with a black man then. His forearms were pecan colored and his lips were superfat and perfect. I think his hair was thinning but it was kept carefully in scrawny dreads. He was adopted. He was wary and closed and seemed untethered. Not crazy. Just without anyone. When we were together he talked and I listened. He talked about what he was getting next from Best Buy or the J.Crew catalogue. He talked about making his record on CD Baby. He wanted some tropical fish. He was long-term housesitting for some friends in one of the nicer neighborhoods where professors and retirees lived. There was wisteria. The house was spacious and felt uninhabited. There was a housemate I never saw but I was loud at night so I was glad I never ran into him. There was a tree in the middle of the house. A big old magnolia. Damon said they hadn't wanted to cut it down when they built it so they built the house around it. The house was in the shape of a square with the center cut out. That was where the tree was, and all the interior walls of the house were glass so you could see it.

He grew giant supremely nourished marijuana plants in a closet in his bedroom, but I didn't know that until I'd been going over there for eight or nine months. The strange part was that I had never even looked in that closet, or asked what was there. I hadn't noticed it but it was right there in the wall, a door with a knob. It was odd because I am the kind that will notice everything in a house and will peek under papers.

There were three transformations: He gave me my first orgasm. We stayed up all night listening to Ben Harper on the expensive fantastic stereo in the living room. We lay on the floor wrapped in a blanket. We kissed and then he pulled my pants off and stretched out on his belly. He held me down so firmly I couldn't scoot away even though in the beginning it was just too much. So much. He had his arms wrapped under my legs and back over and his hands pulling back the lips and he flicked my clit so hard and pointed and precise and sweet. I couldn't do anything but feel it. I didn't know how to help then. He did it all. When it came it was a train, it was heavy and I couldn't do anything but have it. I sang out—I was so loud he covered my mouth even though there was no one in the house. He said I don't think they've been taking care of you have they.

The second was pot. He taught me how to do that. He was beautiful with it. So deliberate. Grinding the buds for the joint, rolling it. The way he sat forward on the couch with his arms balanced on his knees and his handsome fingers handling the paper with such respect and delicacy. So serious. His glasses would slip down his nose a bit while he focused and he would pause and hold the paper trough so still in one hand while he nudged his glasses up with the other. Nothing happened of course the first few times but one afternoon when we were both off we went to the Olive Garden on a date. I was married. I didn't hide it from my husband. Damon and I smoked out before we left his place to go to the restaurant. It was in the car that I finally felt it and I tipped forward and put my hands on my knees and felt warm and good. I felt desperate and so content. I felt like I knew everything about life. I knew what it was. I knew it was real and I knew what real meant. My eyes were closed and I said Oh. Damon said Hey Marie are you good? I didn't say anything. I was thinking about life. He said Hey. I could feel him looking at me. Hey, he said. You got to be able to shake that off. I don't want to shake it off, I said. Sit up, he said. I leaned back but I didn't open my eyes. When we got to the restaurant I didn't want to get out of the car. We sat in the parking lot listening to Dar Williams. The bright rasp of her fingers lifting off the strings connected my ears with my nipples with my cunt. My ears pulsed and my nipples pulsed and my cunt pulsed. I felt the milk and I pushed in on my breasts and thought about my husband and my baby and how much I loved them. Hey, he said. Open your eyes. I looked at him. You ready to go inside? Or what. I'm ready, I said. Okay, he said. You're cool?

I'm great, I said.

We went inside. We sat across from each other with the breadsticks between us. I don't know what we talked about. Everything tasted amazing. He said I sure was occupying a lot of space in his head. I don't think I said much. Olives don't even grow in a garden, I said.

The last one was that night when we got back to his place. We didn't turn on any lights but there was a full moon shining down on the tree in the middle of the house and everything inside was gray and blue. I said I wanted to listen to the Powderfinger album so he turned it on and then he sat down on a barstool with one foot on the floor and one on the bottom rung. I kissed him and pressed my hard breasts against his chest and then I unbuckled his pants and pulled out his cock and I felt such affection for it. Such devotion. It was so big and so fat and so hard and so straight. I kissed the top of it and then I was sucking on him and licking him forever. With so much love. There was nothing but my mouth around him. Nothing else but feeling what he was feeling and giving him what he wanted. I gave myself over to it and I knew what to do. The sounds he made were so genuine and grateful. I was moving with the music. I was performing. Just like that I understood how to be sexy like I'd finally understood what it was to be high and it was as if I had always known even though I hadn't until that night. When he came he curled forward over me and cradled my head and I was wrapped up in the middle of him and I was swallowing it all and I could feel the vibration of his sounds on the back of my head. I stayed there with him far back in my throat after he'd finished and I had swallowed all of it. I waited until he sat up and then I let him go gently and sat back on my heels and looked up at him and wiped my mouth with the back of my hand. Damn, he said. Damn. Where'd you learn to do that? he asked, looking at me with admiration and disbelief. Here, I said.

There was a small room in the hall between the bedrooms. I don't know what it was supposed to be. It didn't have any windows but it wasn't a closet. He had set up his own stereo in there and his guitars were lined up on their stands. There were speakers in each corner and a big beanbag in the middle of the room. After I learned how to get high and suck dick we started going in there at night. He'd light a candle and turn on Jack Johnson or something else mellow. Ani DiFranco. Sometimes Patrice Pike. The Honeytree Lie. One night it was Alanis singing something better than the ironic song and I found her voice and figured out how to give it up to him too. I was lying with my back on the beanbag and my bottom on the carpet and he was inside me and I rode her voice with my pelvis. I let it go. Oh God Marie he said. I let him have all of it and he came and I knocked over the candle with my foot and the flame went out but we didn't do anything about it because we were both having his climax. He passed out right away. I didn't move. I was comfortable in the dark on the beanbag with his weight on me and his cock inside me. I liked it in that room. The smallness of it made me feel right. It was like a secret. Like we had found a place outside of life. Or under it. Away. When You Oughta Know came on I was glad the stereo remote was by my hand so I could skip it without disturbing him. I lay there in the dark listening to her and looking at the dark and smelling his neck. I closed my eyes and cried while she sang. You choose you learn she said. You pray you learn. You ask you learn. I was crying without letting my body move. It was only tears. I was keeping my breathing normal and I wasn't making any sounds but the emotions made the milk come out fast and hot and I couldn't push on them because he was lying on top of me. I hadn't nursed her in over eight hours and there was so much milk. He woke up when he felt it on his chest. I'm leaking, I said. Wow, he said. He got up off me and when he did I could feel all the streams streaking away from my body and he said Whoa! because some of it was still reaching him. I didn't try to stop it because I needed to let the milk go anyway if I wasn't going to feed her. He turned on the overhead light and when he saw that the milk was shooting out and dripping off my body onto the floor he said Hey! Shit! and grabbed his shirt off the floor and covered me with it.

I took what I'd learned back to my husband and taught him how to go down on me. I mean I didn't explain it or anything but I knew what to do with my hips and I knew what to ask for and I discovered that he had a sweet mouth and he loved making me come. He loved me.

———

The morning I didn't get up and pulled a package of saltines out of the drawer of the nightstand and took small bites without raising my head up off the pillow he said Is it mine? I don't know, I said. I could feel him staring at the ceiling. He went with me to Planned Parenthood. If I had known whose it was I would have had it. If it had been Damon's I would have wanted it. If I had known it was my husband's I would have wanted it. But I couldn't want it without knowing.

After that I stopped seeing Damon for a while but my husband seemed older and wise in the saddest way. He didn't want to eat and his cheekbones sharpened. He went for long walks with the baby. One night we had candlelit sex on the floor in the living room. We would have done it on the couch but the couch was covered in clean laundry. Her toys were all over the floor around us. When he came he kicked the door to her little plastic barn and it made the cow stick its

head out with a loud electronic moo. We laughed. The baby
woke up and cried and I went to feed her.

———

I walked out of Chili's one Saturday morning when
Kevin tried to punish me. I worked all the time. Every night
and doubles on the weekends. I would pick up anyone's
shift, anything to get my mind into that gray place. Everyone knew I would work for them if they asked. I had agreed
to take this girl's shift but I didn't realize it was an opener's.
I was supposed to be there at ten fifteen and I got there at
ten forty. I thought I was early because I thought her shift
started at eleven. I still had plenty of time to do all the opening work but Kevin was pissed and told me I couldn't wait
tables. He told me to go stand in the dish pit and take plates
from the servers. When lunch got going and they started
bringing me stacks from their tables each of them asked me
what I was doing there. I was embarrassed and angry and
I thought it was dumb since I never fucked up and I always
came in early and stayed late. I didn't understand how it was
going to teach me anything to stand there in the dish pit. I
was so angry I felt my nose blush and my eyes start to water
so I took off my apron and left it on a stack of clean glasses
on my way out the to-go door.

I went over to Damon's. I had only been seeing him at
work. I would stand close to him while he scooped chips out
of the warmer. He would look at me and raise his eyebrows.
When he opened the door he said What's up. I came in and
we went back to his bedroom. The door of the weed closet

was open and he was in the middle of tending the plants. What?! I said. You didn't know? he asked. No idea, I said. I sat on the bed and watched him. There was a bong on the floor so I picked it up and took a hit. I lay back on the pillow still holding the stem and I imagined someone driving the blunt glass tip of the stem into the hollow of my throat. He came and sat down next to me and picked up the bong and I handed him the stem. So what's happening, he said. I quit, I said. I walked out. I told him why and he took a bubbly hit and while he held the smoke in his mouth he said Kevin's a prick. He lifted his chin and pushed up his glasses and inhaled twice and then he let out the smoke in rings.

We went up into the mountains, to a village outside Toluca, and we built a road. It was as hard as it sounds. Endless scraping in the heat, turning your mouth into your shirtsleeve to try to breathe through the asphalt fumes. Your dad soaked a bandana in water and wrung it out and draped it over his head like a wig, his cap on top to keep it in place. He looked funny but before long we all did it to stay cool. After eight hours we had completed about three feet of road. I was the only girl who had stuck with it all day. The others had stopped after lunch and gone to distribute clothes to the schoolchildren. You're tough, he said, offering me a paper cone of water. I drank it and said I just feel strange around children. We drank more water and then saw our local guide gesturing for us to join the rest of the group to walk back into town, where we were staying. Vámonos, said your dad. He grabbed one side of the water cooler and I took the other.

———

Two years later. I sat on our balcony in a plastic chair and stared at the people in the cars going past. Some of them looked back at me and I wondered if the ones who didn't felt the look and just didn't look back, or if only some people can feel it when others look at them.

I didn't make your dinner, your dad did. You came and sat in my lap while he made your sandwich. Just you in your diaper. Your sunset hair, so long down your tiny back. You sat quietly with me as if we were considering the same thing. He brought you the sandwich on a plastic plate and I held the plate for you. You pointed at the sandwich—thin ham between two soft pieces of brown bread—and said Cut it. Cut it, Mama.

The Dream Café

I was fired from the Dream Café. The lunch rush was over so I was taking my break, sitting in one of the two-person booths with a grilled scone and the crossword. It was a Wednesday, the last day of the week that I bothered to attempt such clues as First PM of Burma (three letters).

Marlo sat down across from me as I put a buttered bite into my mouth. We need to talk, she said. I saw what you did today.

I chewed and swallowed. She told me not to ring them up so I thought it was okay, I said.

Tanya may act like she owns this place but she doesn't. I do. So I'm going to have to let you go, said Marlo.

Whenever anyone says let you go I see myself falling like the girlfriend in *Cliffhanger*. I nodded, wondering how let you go became the way to say You're fired. It sounds like an act of mercy or kindness. Releasing a feral cat after trapping and spaying it.

Do you have anything to say? Marlo asked.

I wasn't sure what she wanted there. For me to grovel? I

knew that what I'd done was sketchy. But I used to let myself be led into that kind of situation—I could see it coming, or feel it, but I went toward it anyway, in some kind of perverted defiance. Tanya had come in for lunch on her day off and we were doing half-price poinsettias to get rid of three gallons of cranberry juice that had been opened but seemed untouched. Marlo had stalked around the place trying to figure out who was responsible but there was no incentive to confess or turn someone in. I was supposed to ring them up before I made them, but I was in a hurry and Tanya was pounding them like shots. Then when I went to ask if she wanted anything else before I brought the check she said How many of these girly drinks did I have? Eight, I said. She whistled. That many, she said. Let's call it five, okay? Maybe you lost count. Since it's been so busy, she said. Okay, I said. Don't worry, I'll take care of you, she said. She looked at my hand, as it lifted her plate off the table. She looked at my arm. I like your—accessorization, she said, twirling her fingers in the air like she was opening a safe. I was wearing six copper bracelets. I could tell their jangling annoyed Marlo but I liked the way they punctuated all my movements.

Tanya had been halfway nice to me, in that beatup way career low-grade hospitality workers have. The ones in whom something has quit, bitterly, and then quit again, resigned. They've made it this far by not fucking up too much or knowing how to manage it when they do, so they're typically proficient if not too shiny. Tanya exhibited the classic mix I've seen in certain individuals who've been in the business for ten years or more: an air of woundedness, of insult, attributable to their prolonged indentured servitude,

combined with an in-spite-of-it pride in their personal performance of the job. Especially when new people showed up.

So she'd taken me under her dubious scraggly wing. She
was tall and butch. This was a restaurant on the edge of the
gayborhood so I was in the heterosexual minority. Tanya
sometimes cooked and sometimes waited tables. Her face
was usually gray, like someone on the verge of death. Even
behind the line, where it got so hot Nacho and Fili would put
cornstarch on their balls to keep them from sticking too bad,
her face didn't heat up. She showed me how to carry three
glasses in one hand so I wouldn't need a tray to get drinks
to a four-top. She told me which bussers would roll your silverware for five bucks. Does that look appetizing to you?
she said to me one day when I was so slammed I couldn't
get back to the window to run a hot cobbler before the à la
mode had melted into a sad moat. I was going to drop it on
the table anyway but she stopped me. Not really, I said. So
don't take it out, she said. Wait a few minutes and I'll get you
a new one. Those two won't even notice. She could see my
table over the kitchen line—two older gay men on the same
side of the booth, clearly having an intense relationship talk.

She pulled the cobbler from the window. What do I tell
Marlo? I asked. Don't, she said. I do the count anyway. It
was a spill.

Thanks, I said. I wasn't sure what to make of the favor.
Sometimes I thought she was flirting with me but I ignored it.
Occasionally people—customers and new servers—thought
I might be gay because I worked there and I didn't try very
hard with my face or my hair. I have big square hands I never
grew into. They were meant for a farm or a piano. Or for

carrying four full-size entrée plates up one flight of stairs, down two steps, up a ramp, through a door, around a fat clueless man waiting for a table on the lawn, and finally down a last set of stairs into the outdoor recessed patio. I never dropped anything there. That was years ago and I still feel like I need to knock on wood when I say that.

So many times I ran that gauntlet. If I were to advise someone going into the service industry, my second suggestion after Don't would be Walk through the place and look for the tables farthest from the kitchen. You'll probably be stuck in that station for a couple months. Imagine walking from wherever that is all the way back to the kitchen for extra salad dressing. Now imagine it eighteen more times, and that's just for one table. You may think you'll be waiting tables but really your job is to walk fast in a circle for six to eight hours every day. Don't work somewhere with stairs, steps, ramps, outdoor seating, small water glasses, or kids' menus.

The Dream Café had all those things. I never dropped food but I did lose a credit card once. On busy brunches I could have fifty or sixty covers in two hours and there was no stopping no matter what. The managers told us Don't be afraid to ask for help, that's what we're here for but it wasn't that I was afraid. I didn't have time to ask for help. They were a beautiful family. The Dream Café was popular with trainers and athletes and otherwise regular people who spent more than two hours a day working out, because the menu was full of organic and vegetarian and local and whole before that was common. She looked like an aerobics instructor and he looked like a linebacker. She was tiny, and exquisitely proportioned. Every time she lifted a forkful of seasonal fruit to her mouth all of her elegantly defined arm muscles flexed slightly, as if eager and then disappointed that more was not being asked of them. He wore his Oakleys the entire time they were there, and he had to sit in the chair like he was riding a short horse, legs spread, knees almost touching the ground. Excuse me, miss, he said, after I had dropped off the check, picked up the check, run the card, stuffed the vouchers back in the book, and dropped it off again with a Thanks so much, take care, and they had begun the process of packing up their baby, who was undoubtedly beautiful too but could barely be found in the middle of a gigantic machine that looked more like a Bowflex than a stroller. I was seating a table behind them when I felt a light touch on my elbow. I turned around. Yes sir? I said. The woman was lifting the napkins, the plates, the coffee mugs, the sugar caddy. It's not here, she said. Our credit card, said the man. It wasn't in here. He handed me the check presenter. I opened it, like he could have missed it somewhere in the see-through plastic pocket that said PLEASE COME AGAIN. I saw that he had already filled out the voucher. Their brunch was seventy dollars, more than you could ever hope for from a two-top with a baby. He'd left me fifteen, indicating firmly that someone had taught him twenty percent. Oh no, I said. Do you think it could have fallen out? he asked. Yes, I'm sure that's it, I said. Let me go look. I got down on my knees and looked under the table first, hoping they had dropped it, but it wasn't there. Did you put it back in your wallet? she asked him. No, he said, don't you think that's the first place I looked? I'm sorry, I said, I'll be right back. I ran-walked through the patio, scrutinizing the ground and the potted plants lining the walkway. Fucking shitfuck, I said under my breath. Excuse me, said a young man in a hoodie and flip-flops with a party of three other guys in the same hangover brunch costume, could we get some drinks here? I pretended I didn't hear him. Guess not, I heard him say. No credit card. I crashed into the back station where I'd run their card. Craig was standing there voiding something for someone. What now, he said, as if I were always walking up to him in crisis. Quite a few of my colleagues were, in fact, always in crisis, even when they had only one table, but I was usually able to handle my own shit well enough to help those people out. I certainly wasn't one of them. Has anyone found a credit card? I asked. No, why? he said. Because I lost one. What do you mean, you lost one? he said, pausing in his heavy poking of the touchscreen to turn his face to me. I mean I can't find it anywhere. I dropped off the check and it's gone. What table? he said. Forty-three, I said. The big guy. We looked out the door toward forty-three. They were arguing. I wondered if we would have to comp the tab and there would go one of my biggest tips of the day. You're kidding, said Craig. They own the Smoothie King up the street. Did you look everywhere out there? Yes! I said. Maybe he put it in his wallet, said Craig, still staring at him. God, I'd love to put something in his wallet, he murmured. He looked, I said. Could you please go talk to them? I have four other tables out there. I can't go back if I have to go past him without his card, I said. I'll talk to them, but you better keep looking, he said.

Craig was one of those people who worked out more

than two hours a day. He spent at least four in the gym next door to the Dream before he came in to work. Even Sundays. He drank three gallons of water during a shift. His upper body was ripped but he was kind of short and he had bad teeth. He smoked a lot. He had the angular weatherworn cheekbones of a shepherd from a hard land. Managing a restaurant is probably somewhat like being a shepherd. Doing the same thing every day. Same territory, over and over. Watching mammals eat. Keeping everyone in line.

I looked all over the POS while I watched him out the door, talking to them. I saw him laugh. I tried to remember where I was on all my other tables now that an interminable digression had broken my rhythm. I rang up two orders and grabbed a water pitcher and headed back into the breach, squeezing behind Craig to get to my station, putting him between me and the linebacker like a body shield. I'm so sorry, I said to forty-two, have you had a chance to decide?

No one found a credit card anywhere. Everyone was put on the lookout. After the madness Tanya and I looked through every single check presenter. I even got Nacho to check the men's room. Nothing. When I went to turn in my cashout Craig said Why did you close out forty-three? Because I had the voucher, I said. Yeah but we never found the card. We can't make them pay the bill if we lost their card, he said to me like I was trying to fleece them and he was their good-hearted defender. So what do I do? I said. I'll comp it, just give me a second, he said. He was chomping through an enormous pile of steamed broccoli while he entered cashouts in the office.

I sat down in a booth to wait. I felt the clock pressing on me. Now I had less than two hours to rest at home before I had to be at the Italian restaurant where I worked nights. I closed my eyes. Can you help run some stock? barked Marlo. No, I thought. Sure, I said. If it got close to one hour there wasn't much point in going home, and I kept my other uniform in my car because sometimes that happened. But sometimes even if I could only be home for five minutes I would make the drive. I would sit on the floor in the bathroom and close the door, even though I lived alone. To feel like there was something between me and all that for a few moments.

As I was restocking some coffee mugs Craig called out that he had comped the bill and I could rerun my cashout. Can you back out the sales? I asked. He looked at me again like I was the wolf in the darkness. No, he said. We still had the cost. I know, but I have to tip out on money I didn't get tipped on, I said. Sorry, he said, refilling his water bottle from a gallon jug under the desk in the office. The office was next to the back door and as I was standing there trying to calculate how much I had paid to wait on them Pedro the busser walked up to the door with a bus tub so full the mound of dirty plates obscured most of his face. I took a step toward the door to open it for him and as I held it I happened to look down. There it was, lodged in the frame of the door. Their black Citi MasterCard. Craig! I yelled. Don't yell! he hissed from the office. I found it! I said. Look! He stepped out of the office. What the hell? he said. I pointed at the card. Seriously? he said skeptically. No, I said, I've had it in my pocket all this time because I just wanted to screw myself, but I changed my mind and stuck it in the door so I could look like a moron too.

What is going on here? said Marlo from behind me. You need to watch your tone.

I didn't mean it like that, Craig said to me, ignoring her. I just meant—this place, he said, shaking his head.

I'm sorry, I said to both of them.

Marlo was one who never backed down, but she performed the duties of power awkwardly, like a child playing teacher. Bossing people around while checking with herself every minute to see if she really meant it. She said If you're not helping out you should go home, and walked outside. We watched her griping at Zeke for not refilling his pepper shakers.

She hates me, I said to Craig.

No she doesn't, said Craig. Her husband has Crohn's disease. He'd be super cute if he wasn't shaped like a chopstick with a head.

———

Do you have anything to say? Marlo repeated.

Well, I'd like to keep my job, I said to Marlo, who was already leaning out of the booth. It took me too long to come up with that unconvincing response but it was all I could think of to mask the panic. I'd looked outside and indulged the thought of never having to fix another wobbly patio table with sugar packets or check presenters for a split second but I didn't know anyone in Dallas then except for the people at my restaurants. I was a month behind on my car payment.

Sometimes I would pick up a dinner shift at the Italian place if they had scheduled me off just because they served a family meal for all the waiters and kitchen staff before service.

I'm sorry, she said. You were stealing. You're lucky I'm only firing you.

I nodded and looked down at my crossword. First PM of Burma. Marlo walked away. I thought I might cry so I dug the fingernails of my right hand into my left arm until it stopped. I left my plate with the scone and my glass of water and the crossword on the table and walked slowly to my car. I called Marshall, my boss at the Italian place, and asked for the night off. He said Sure, because I had never asked. You work too much, he said. Enjoy it.

Then I called Tanya. They fired me, I said. What the fuck?! she said. That fucking bitch.

She didn't ask why they fired me. Come over, she said. Have a beer. That just sucks.

I didn't really want to hang out with Tanya but I said Okay. It felt like school was out for the summer. Towel thrown, game over.

We drank Michelob Ultras. She had a generic one-bedroom apartment in Uptown, the kind they put corporate guys in for long projects. It was nice enough only if you knew you were going home before long. She put on some weird techno house music through her computer and we sat on her couch watching the screen saver—colored straws of light spinning and lengthening. She said You're too good for that place anyway. She touched her fingers to my hair and pretended like she wasn't doing anything. I looked down at her other hand wrapped around her beer. Something was wrong with her thumb. It looked like soggy bread. She saw me looking and said, Bar rot. I know it's gross. Sorry. She stood up so I couldn't see her thumb anymore. I've just been doing this too long, she said. She took off her shirt and pulled the band out of her hair so it fell around her shoulders but it still looked mullety. She undid her bra with one hand and let it fall off. She wasn't pretty but she did have attractive breasts. I had never seen another woman's breasts until then. I came from such modest people. She kissed me. I didn't want to be there. So stupid. She unbuttoned my pants. I felt her breasts with both my hands. I didn't know what to do with them. I was fascinated but I was kneading them like dough. She looked annoyed. Take these off, she said, jerking on my belt so I fell back on the couch. She yanked off my pants and my panties and then her gruff momentum snagged. You don't shave? she said. No, I said. Should I?

How do I get to it in all that? she asked, waving imprecisely toward my groin. I guess I should go, I said. I have to work. At least I still have one job.

I stood up and pulled on my pants. I left my underwear on her floor. Thanks for the beer, I said.

Hey, wait! she said. It's just—she looked around the room. You should come into Monica's for a drink sometime. On me, she said, raising her hands like she didn't have a weapon. Her tits splayed out and then swung back together. I'm there every night but Sunday, she said. See you later, I said.

If I wasn't at work I felt like I should go be with my daughter. I got in my car. I put the key in the ignition. Ana, I said. Ana.

I hate flying. There's always a moment somewhere in the middle of the flight when I feel shocked that I have put myself there, thirty-five thousand feet off the ground. Strapped into a metal coffin. After I moved out I kept having a similar sensation, especially when I was driving home from work. Like there was nothing I could do to get back to ground except crash or stay the course.

It was almost four. I went to my apartment where I lived without Ana and got into bed with my clothes on. I fell asleep aching for her. Her body was the only real thing. Her voice.

———

I woke up because my phone was ringing. Dream, said the caller ID. It looked dark outside. You never want to answer a call from your restaurant. Someone is sick or no-call no-showed and they want you to come in, or they're just extra busy and they want you to come in, or it's dead and they're telling you not to come in when you really needed the money. I didn't answer. I don't work there, I said to my phone. I turned over and tried to go back to sleep. The phone said it was 6:47 a.m. It rang again. Dream. I didn't answer. I went back to sleep.

———

I woke up again in the afternoon and remembered I was fired. I had two new voicemails, both from Craig. In the first one he was asking me where I was because I was supposed to open and Elaine was there already. Elaine came in every weekday for breakfast. We didn't open until seven but she was always waiting in her Maybach in the parking lot by quarter till, and if she saw us inside setting up sometimes she would come in early. She drank an entire pitcher of iced tea—she told us to leave the pitcher on the table—and had one piece of sausage and one sliced avocado. She tipped well, almost always five on five. She reviewed documents for an hour and drank her tea and you gave her a to-go cup with the bill.

In the second message he said he'd spoken with Marlo and she'd told him I was fired. He said he told her they needed me, and then he said So you're not fired. I'm sorry about that but please come back to work tomorrow. That's when I cried. Because I was relieved I wasn't fired. Because I hated that I wasn't fired. Because I was crying over that shit job. Because of Tanya's thumb. I got up and went into the bathroom and took my box cutter out of the drawer and sliced a horizontal stripe across my thigh. Fuck you! I said to myself. I sliced another stripe below the first one. Suck it up, you whiny little turd, I said. Or what, I screamed, cutting a third line in. Blood was running down my leg and pooling at the top of my sock but the cuts didn't hurt as much as the crackling in my brain, or seeing my face in the mirror.

———

If you want to keep working here you need to wear some makeup, said Marlo. You always look tired. Put some concealer on those, she said, looking toward my head but not into my eyes. I never had acne as an adolescent or ever until I started working in restaurants. At the Dream Café it got worse. I was always breaking out around my mouth even though I was careful to never touch my face. And I want you to wear a long-sleeved shirt under your Dream shirt. What are all those marks?

Burns, I said. There were dots and dashes of scar tissue up and down the inside and outside of both of my arms. They were uniformly spaced and reminded me of a fretboard. And other things. The deepest ones took several years to heal. Or fully scar, or whatever the curing process is called. So some of them were still pink and bright.

I bought three waffle-knit thermal undershirts at Goodwill and kept working at the Dream Café.

———

What are all those marks? asked Zeke. At first I'd thought he was gay because of the way he walked but it turned out he was just a nerd. We started doing my crossword together and sharing food. Together we could do the Thursday and sometimes the Friday. I had been at the Dream for nine months then and of the servers he and Tanya were the only ones who'd been there longer. Eventually we went back to his place after a brunch shift. His place was disgusting. It was an efficiency at Lovers and Skillman and it was filthy and dark. Everything was black. I still take wide detours around that intersection because I don't want to think about it. There was one window but he had covered it with a blackout curtain. He had two cats and it smelled like cat shit. His bed was gritty from litter that came off the cats' paws. They're burns, I said. So you're one of those, he said. One of what? I said. His computer chimed and he got up off the bed where we had been making out. Hold on, he said. This girl in Japan died. We're having an online wake for her. Someone you knew? I asked. Yes, he said. I mean, just online, but we in-game chatted all the time. He typed something and then he came back to the bed, which was only one step from the computer desk. We started kissing again and then we moved on. I went into my bathroom and shut the door and turned on the water. I changed the carpet to be fluffy and white and gave myself a big white robe and smooth legs. I erased all the rust marks from around the drain in the bathtub and erased all the dull gray that wasn't anything but old calcified faded grime until the bathtub was spotless. Then I just got rid of that bathtub and started over with a brand-new claw-foot that no one had ever bathed in but me. I took out the toilet and put it in one of those tiny rooms that has its own door. I put in a couch next to the bathtub so I could lie on the couch and watch the water run. I made the bathtub deeper so the water could run longer. I upholstered the couch in the fluffy white carpet so it felt like I was still lying on the floor. Hey, said Zeke. Marie. Hey.

I opened my eyes. Did you come? he said. No, I said. Do you think these are too big? he asked. He held up a string of four plastic beads the size of large grapes. What are they? I asked. You've never tried anal beads before? he said. No, I said. What about just anal? he asked. Once or twice, I said.

It was really only once. When my husband and I went into the bayou between New Orleans and Baton Rouge for a week of intensive marriage counseling after I started burning myself. My parents paid for it and kept the baby. It didn't work but we did have anal sex and the woman counselor gave me a recipe for oatmeal blueberry pancakes that I still make. When we went home no one wanted me to be alone with the baby anymore and my husband wanted to go to college. She was weaned by then so my mother started watching her at night while he was in class. We filed for divorce and he gave me half his first student loan check so I could move to Dallas, where I rented an apartment that had a $1 move-in special. I didn't have a job and I didn't know anyone.

You'll like these better, said Zeke. Turn over. I remember his fingernails had those white marks on them that your grandmother says means how many lies you've told.

The third day in Mexico we follow our guide single file through a forest and up the side of a mountain. At the top is a trout farm, which means a beautiful clear shallow stream flowing in narrow rows lined with round stones. There is a thatched shelter with long wooden tables where we sit and rest. We are three hours up and we can see all of the DF shimmering below. We are high enough that it looks almost like it did from the plane.

Our guide skims trout from the stream with a net and carries them over to an old woman, who cooks them whole over an open flame while she makes tortillas. The fire is in the ground under a grate. The fish smoke on the grate and the tortillas cook in an iron skillet. She squats, turning the fish and shaping the tortillas and looking at nothing. At intervals she scoops fat out of a plastic Big Gulp cup and flicks it off her fingers onto the skillet. When the fish are cooked she places each one on a tin plate and motions for us to come get them, one by one. We say Gracias, and she says Dios te bendiga to each one of us, looking into our eyes. When it is my turn I see that she has not been looking at nothing but I see that she knows I thought that she was.

We sit at the tables and eat. The fish still have their heads and their tails. I have never tasted anything so good. There are no napkins so your dad takes his bandana out of his pocket and we share it to wipe the grease off our faces.

When everyone has eaten, they tell us to take our plates downstream from the fish and rinse them. I stand and take your dad's plate and mine and step out from under the thatch, but as I move into the sun I look at the old woman and fall.

I don't know that I fall. This is what your dad tells me later. The sun, the mountain, says the guide. It does that. One minute okay, then—*pff,* he says, making a motion with his hand like he's letting go of an invisible dove. When I open my eyes the first thing I see is your dad's face, and he looks so concerned I think If I could just stay here with him, looking at me like that.

———

You are strong. My father calls you Little Boot because when you fall you never cry. You can read when you are four and I ask you to help me memorize the parts of the cow. You have a lisp and I tell you to say brisket over and over just so I can hear it. But when you fall asleep I go into the bathroom and do lines off the map of the steer. I read about the difference between Kobe and Wagyu and I feel replete with the beauty of your small self. Just imagining it—the everything of you—my body tingles and quivers like the air inside a guitar. I am freezing. I get into bed with you. You like staying with me because you get to sleep with me. You are so warm but I can't stop shivering. I feel a soaring bliss—I adore you—I feel a plummeting ugly resentment—I am a pile of shit falling endlessly down a dark shaft, I am the hate that hurled the shit and the fear inside the hurled shit. If you slip out one stitch in your brain high and low are the same. I don't realize I've said that aloud until you turn over to face me. Mama, you say, what's wrong? I see in your face the deepest empathy and your mouth pulls down. I realize nothing else is happening in your life at this moment. You are here with your mother who is crying, so you cry too.

Intermezzo

J immy plays at The Restaurant three nights a week, from seven until eleven or until the last guest leaves, whichever comes first. When he sees the last guests cross the threshold of the door out of the dining room into the lobby he'll stop in the middle of his chill Jobim or his John Williams show tune, right in the middle of an arpeggio, stand up, shut the lid, grab his bag, walk out. The effect is as abrupt as turning off a stereo except that sometimes the last note he played drifts there in the air, along with the smells of butter and salt.

The piano sits on a dais in the middle of the open kitchen, right in front of the dining room. It's a black Yamaha concert grand, and too nice to be in The Restaurant's kitchen. When Lissandri hired him eight years ago Jimmy didn't mention that, afraid he would sell it when he learned its worth, since the rate Jimmy was offered to play there was less than he was used to. That was right after Valentino's burned down, and he needed the work so much he didn't bother to argue with a man he knew from *D Magazine* to be one of Dallas's wealthiest. Valentino's had been a great gig, five nights a week and just two blocks from his M Street bungalow. He walked there, he didn't wear a tie, the bartender poured him a glass of Chianti as soon as the rush was over. Best of all the owners liked to close early and often. That gave him plenty of downtime, and freed up New Year's Eve for lucrative one-offs at mansions in Preston Hollow or hotel galas or even, once, he made a thousand dollars playing for Emmitt Smith and his wife while they sat on their couch and watched the ball drop.

Jimmy had to drive into Uptown to play at The Restaurant, and the valets were stingy with their spots so he parked his minivan on the street somewhere in the neighborhood. It was supposed to be a nice part of town, all the most expensive restaurants and condos, but his driver's-side mirror had been broken off once before he started folding it in, and the managers wouldn't let the girl employees leave at the end of the night without a man to walk them out. Jimmy had to wear a suit and tie but he left the top button of his shirt unbuttoned, and sometimes he wore the same suit and tie all week. He saw the servers being reprimanded for wrinkled sleeves or dirty aprons or ties tied sloppily and prepared an excuse for his unbuttoned button that had something to do with mobility and piano playing, but no one ever said anything to him. Often he had trouble finding a parking spot near the restaurant and this frustrated him until he settled into it as a believable excuse for being a few minutes late every time he played, and sat in the van for a short spell even when he found a space on the first try. No one seemed to notice that either, and when he did walk in he made sure it was with the same quick keen purpose every night. As if he couldn't wait to get in there and play.

His second night in The Restaurant he'd closed the keyboard lid at eleven and left his bag of charts on the dais while he stepped into the bar. He asked the bartender—who also lived in the M Streets and whom he knew as a patron of Valentino's, and who had done him the favor of telling Lissandri he knew a piano man, he knew the best piano man in town—for a glass of whatever Italian they were pouring. He took a stool at the end of the bar and had sipped only two sips when he felt an arm around his shoulder and there was the man himself on his left, saying Buddy you're here to play not drink all right?

All right, all right, so he played. He was a little late and he was quick to leave but he played. He played the requisite mix of big band and lounge and pop and he played Happy Birthday four or five times a night when the servers took out chocolate soufflés with candles in them. For kids he played The Rainbow Connection and songs from *Beauty and the Beast* and *The Little Mermaid*. He played the Elton John, the Billy Joel, the Norah Jones their parents asked for. Hey sure I know Your Song! Comin right up! Come Away With Me? Sure I know that! You got it ma'am! When the guests asked he played the Jim Brickman, which he resented even more than the Cielito Lindo he played for Hank Earl Jackson, a gigantic six-foot-seven alcoholic with a head the size of a steer's who owned an eponymous bar in the Fort Worth stockyards. Hank Earl's was more than a bar, it was an A-list venue for any country act that came to Texas, and while Hank Earl was famous for it that wasn't how he made his money. He was an oil man, like Lissandri was an investment man, their nightlife ventures only toys, things they did with the money they'd already made. Jimmy had been playing in restaurants long enough to know that actually making money from a restaurant was hard to do.

Hank Earl never requested Cielito Lindo until late in the evening, after he'd had at least two or three bottles of chardonnay poured over ice. Cielito Lindo was a cow-herding song, a ranchero song, a mariachi song, and often Jimmy would hear a tired Mexican cook behind him sing along, *Ay, ay, ay, ay,* while he cleaned the broiler. Over the years Hank Earl had requested the song almost every time he was in the place, which was at least three or four times a week since he lived across the street in the Hotel Fitzandrew. His driver picked him up in the porte cochere at the hotel, made a right out of the driveway and then an immediate left into The Restaurant's porte cochere, repeating the trip in reverse at the end of the night. Hank Earl had vomited, pissed, and passed out in the back of the town car on the way back across the street so many times that the driver, Hector, told Jimmy he was grateful when only one of the three occurred, and would have chosen piss if he could, since the man was impossible to wake or move and at least some of the piss would stay on Hank Earl's pants. If Jimmy had found a prime spot on the street in front of The Restaurant, near where Hector waited with the town car, Jimmy and Hector would chat sometimes when Jimmy stepped out for his break at nine, to smoke his pipe in the minivan. He would sit in the driver's seat smoking his pipe with the window rolled down, listening to Mose Allison.

There are two other piano men who work for The Restaurant, Ted and Ed. He knows Ted, who subbed for him at Valentino's and plays Pearl Jam and Prince covers at the height of service when he thinks no one will notice. Marie notices, Jimmy respects her for noticing even when she is so busy it takes everything to not fuck up. She notices and reports that Ted and Ed are nothing. She says Some of the other servers don't even know who's Ted and who's Ed. Ted has his gimmicks and Ed his Delilah bullshit, she says. You're not a radio show and you're not background, you're a musician. This is how they started talking at first, when Marie was new. Chef didn't like it when the servers stood with their backs to the dining room so she'd step up onto the dais next to him and look out at the guests, standing properly with her hands behind her straight back, in the ready meerkat posture Chef approved. He played whole concerts for her between requests. There was a Bud Powell night and a Chick Corea night and a Hank Jones night. After a few months he started quizzing her. When she swooped by with four steaks up her arm she'd say Ray Charles or Nat Cole as she passed. More often than not she was right. He didn't register surprise at this, only delight. He had a two-note laugh that bounced like a rimshot and cracked him into talking about her like she was a racehorse, She's a winner, ladies and gentlemen! Look at her go! Jimmy would you put all your money on me for the next one, she'd say. You betcha, sister, you betcha, I got one comin at ya, try this on, he'd say. He ran through everything he knew of jazz, R&B, blues, and Broadway before he started in on his classical repertoire, which wasn't a great soundtrack for The Restaurant so he meted it out slowly.

You're not gonna collect much hiding the tip jar under the lid like that, Chopin, she'd said once, and gone to move it out where people could see it. It was a snifter from the bar that lived on the far end of the soundboard. Ted and Ed would take it from its place there and put it up on top by the music stand, level with their heads—you looked at them, you'd see the glass there. Ed even put a twenty-dollar bill in it each night to make it look like somebody already appreciated him. But Jimmy stopped her from moving it. No, no, he said, serious, don't. I'm just playing for you.

She rolled her eyes at that but he meant it, a little. He never would take money from people, would act like he was unable to lift his fingers from the keys to receive it but they would set it on the music stand anyway; sometimes Hank Earl gave him nothing for Cielito Lindo, sometimes a tenner he'd stuff in the snifter with a Thankee, Billy, thankee. Once he stiff-legged it up to the dais, a man who knew his size to be potentially lethal if he stumbled and corrected that with slower movements rather than less drink. He had his glass of chardonnay in one hand and set it on the edge of the piano top by the music stand. Though it wasn't Jimmy's piano he didn't need to see it treated like that, it was enough that the full-size quilted cover had been misplaced or stolen and the keys, especially in the oppressive mug of the summer months, had a film of filmy kitchen air on them. He was playing some Nina Simone right then, Mississippi Goddam, and he cut down to just that frenetic train-ride bass line so he could pick up the glass with his right hand, saying Yes sir what can I do you for, Mr. Jackson? to Hank Earl, who said Nothing nothing I just want—just here—give you some—preciate you you know—while he steadied himself against the piano to pull his money clip from inside his jacket and then tried to dislodge some bills from it. The bills looked new and stuck together and to save face he decided to make it appear as though he had always intended to give the piano man all of them and he dropped the entire clip in the snifter. There that's for you, that's for you, you're the best, tell me your name again? It's Jimmy! Jimmy LaRosa! But I can't take that, don't give me your money, I play for the music, the music and you, they already pay me! Take it back! he yelled over the music and Chef's call for Hands! And Somebody get me Art! and the expo's order to dale gas a la treinta y cinco and the ever-ascending elevator of sound, the heavy machine parts of three eight-hundred-degree broilers and the popping of four fryers and forty clattering pans and pots and bowls and six clicking-airlock slamming walk-in doors and a couple of microwave timer bells and hundreds of Saturday-night conversations all trying to make the restaurant go, go, get to a good time. Nah, nah! said Hank Earl, reaching for the glass of chardonnay Jimmy was holding suspended in air like a single-use flashbulb. Just as he found the stem of the glass, just as he was feeling up the stem like a blind man, like alcohol had risen six feet three inches in his body to leave only his forehead dry, a tide coming in to wash away sight, just as he was getting a better grip on the bowl of the glass before he could shift his weight back upright, a busser knocked a plate off the service station and the ceramic shattered on the kitchen's tile floor and Hank Earl's sixty-six-year-old hand jerked away from him like a dead chicken and sloshed the chardonnay onto Jimmy's lapel. Jimmy kept playing with his left, had never quit playing, even knew where he was in the unplayed vocal (Tennessee). Whoa sir! he said, You okay there? and that's when Marie came out of the dishroom with a stack of clean salad bowls and set them down in the first wrong place on the dessert line to come over and take the glass from Jimmy and lead the big man back to his booth, holding the tablecloth out of the way while he sat down. She returned with a linen and dabbed Jimmy's lapel and soaked up the pool of wine that had collected in the depression of the leather piano bench against Jimmy's thigh. The track lights in the kitchen prismed off all the stainless steel behind him, twinkling the three fake diamond solitaires in Marie's left ear. No one ever had reason to be that close to him while he played. Jimmy had taken up Nina's melody right when the glass had been removed from his hand and now Marie said This is a show tune but the show hasn't been written for it yet, right Jimmy? What a fucking clown that guy! I'm sorry! Don't worry about it, sweetheart, he said, don't worry about it.

Part Two

Suck It

Suck it is Danny's favorite phrase, which he employs as a general greeting. Sometimes he inflects it as a question: Suck it? Directed at a female, it might often be appended: Suck it, sista. This is only for staff members, of course; our patrons will more likely get an egregiously enthusiastic What's up, my brother? accompanied by a hand-shake/backslap combination. (If you're one of his friends you might receive a more sincere What's up, my fucking brother?) Egregious enthusiasm is Danny's trademark—he can transmit his buzz and momentum to anyone at will. This is called charisma. His charisma—any charisma, I suppose—is entirely performance, yet in being never more nor less than a performer he somehow remains endearingly genuine. He might embrace a beautiful woman, kiss her on both cheeks, escort her to the bar—What do you like, sister, what do you want? Cosmo? Martini? Chardonnay? Tequila? Tongue kiss? That's what I thought—Ethan, get my lover here a glass of Mer Soleil, thank you brother—Good to see you, love—and as soon as he spins around to answer your question mutter Dirty whore, suck it.

Almost every question must be brought to Danny, because it's his restaurant. These people want a booth instead of a table, ask Danny. You want Friday off this week, ask Danny. The guy said his steak looked more medium than rare and he wants a different one, better check with Danny. Music's too loud, lights are too low, the room's too cold, tell Danny. You want to go to Silver City, ask Danny—he's king there and she'll fuck you for real in a back room at his word. You want tickets to the game or an eight o'clock reservation at Tei Tei, which doesn't take eight o'clocks—Danny will work it out for you. You need a bump, ask Danny—but not until after service, he never starts till almost everybody's out of the building.

Most nights he gets it from the undocumented Mexican and Salvadoran bussers and dishwashers. The Mexicans are usually from Guanajuato, some from Yucatán—the Yucas have a reputation for being lazy, the Guanajuatans for being easygoing and hardworking. Sometimes on his day off Danny comes up to the restaurant, ostensibly to check on us and grace the regulars with his presence like a politician, but he's also there to pick something up. He'll say to me Pablo working? Get me sixty? and I'll say Okay boss. I pick up a stack of dirty plates and silverware and head into the dish room, where I unload them and then hold up three fingers for only Pablo, who is polishing Bordeaux glasses, to see. He nods with his eyes. A few minutes later I'll come back to wash my hands or run some stock out to the line and he'll discreetly slip me a tiny square package, three twenty-

bags wrapped up tight in a piece of paper towel. I'll wait for
Danny to come find me, or sometimes he'll ask me to put
it under a Le Volte bottle. The Le Volte is a Chianti in the
uppermost corner of the French/Italian wine bin wall; I'm
too short to reach it, so I have to climb up on a chair without being seen. If he pays me I pass the three twenty-dollar
bills along to Pablo—back in the spring he used to ask me to
front it for him and bring it to him somewhere, like the W
or the alley behind the Fitz. I rarely have money I don't need
to spend immediately on something or other, so sometimes
I had to borrow from someone else to get it for him. The
first few times he gave me extra cash when he paid me back,
which I think was supposed to seal me into the whole thing,
but since I quit using I've just been asking the bussers for it.
They know it's for him, and somehow he knows I don't want
to front it anymore, so he settles up with them when he's
back in the restaurant. I hate this arrangement, because I'm
both too timid and too interested in protecting my income
to beg off, and the bussers are barely making a living as it is.
They live in one-bedroom apartments with five other people
and share broken-down cars and every one of them has a
morning job in a different restaurant.

Lately they've been coming down harder on me. There's
something wrong with Pablo's eyes; he has kind of a flat
face, like you see in the pictures of fetal alcohol syndrome
victims, and his pupils are strange. The top half of each is a
cloudy blue, and the bottom half is an opaque dark, so when
he stares at me and says Tellen, tellen Danny que necesita
pagar, tellen Danny he pay, okay? Ten. Diez. I feel disarmed
by his aberrant, unreadable gaze. He tells me in Spanish,

then in English, then he holds up how many fingers to make sure I get it.

My friend Calvin says they're going to start cutting it worse for him, that even though he's their boss they won't tolerate it. We agree that he makes too much money to do it like this, that if he wants it he should just pay for it. Either give me the cash or get right with them straightaway.

Suck it is his favorite, but not by much—we joke that he has Tourette's syndrome, and I wouldn't be surprised if it were true. He might be looking over the seating chart for the night, trying to puzzle out how he can possibly fit another six-top in at seven thirty, and run through a litany like Suck it shit fuck cock 'n' balls shit fuck fuck fuck fuck suck it. He might hang up the phone after sweetly giving a stranger detailed directions and declare Filthy cunt whore suck my cock may I help you?

Every night he makes snap public-relations decisions with a ferocity that is unquestionable and an accuracy that is never less than dead-on. He is a fast-talking Italian fox from the Bronx who can get his way with anyone, can make any Mur feel like a VIP, and thus has been the general manager of a multimillion-dollar-grossing fine-dining steakhouse since he was twenty-four.

(*Mur* is a term that denotes any individual "we don't know." A Mur is just a regular customer, no one deserving of special treatment. This fairly benign significance is the standard, though it might also be used more pejoratively, to indicate that the individual is a nobody, a chump, a tool— all of which in turn signify primarily an absence of wealth.

Example: Honey-love, see those Murs hangin out in the fuckin doorway over there? Would you please take them in to twenty fucking seven. I once inquired about the etymology of Mur, and Danny said that he and his buddy, who is the general manager at our sister restaurant Il Castello, used to know a guy named Murray when they were kids growing up in the Bronx. Murray was a social misfit, soft or naive in some unforgivable way that inspired them to refer to any such person as a Murray, and later simply a Mur.)

But Danny is blowing his crystalline mind four square inches of shittily cut cocaine at a time, night after night. The urgency in his voice when he calls up the restaurant on his days off to ask me to get it for him—well, last night all he said was Four. Now.

———

Danny's appetite is the spirit of the place: the excesses of an entire microculture are concentrated in his one body. We are accustomed to businessmen arriving with clients whom they want to impress, we are accustomed to those businessmen spending our weekly incomes on several bottles of fine wine alone, we are accustomed to a per-person average that can linger fatly around $300. We are accustomed to Danny's binges, his unbelievable gluttony. He routinely fucks women in the restaurant—once there was a pink lacy thong on the floor by the trash can in the office on a Sunday, and he came up to The Restaurant with a friend, even though it was his day off. They were already out of control with their high and they were there for me to get them some more. Danny told the friend my name and he said Ooooh! and looked at me as if he cherished me, because Danny must have told him earlier who was going to help them along. While they were crashing around the office, laughing and pushing and glowing and shrieking, Danny told me and the wine manager how he had fucked this one girl by the trash can last night (above the thong on the floor, he reenacted his thrusting), and how he then fucked her friend in the same place. I guess that one wasn't wearing underwear, or kept it on.

There is a kind of partying undertaken by people of my age and station on birthdays, or on other momentous occasions such as the losing of a job. The kind of partying that leaves one wrecked for days, sometimes close to death. The kind of partying that concludes with the unconscious body of the individual being arranged by any remaining friends in such a way that it can be trusted not to aspirate vomit. This is the kind of partying that lingers so badly it causes one to leave off for another year or so. This is also the kind of partying that Danny rips through several times a week.

He was in the hospital last month. No one could remember a day when Danny didn't come in—in seven years he's never been out sick. He's been in all fucked up, for sure, but he maintains better than most people who aren't fucked up, so a hush came over us when they said he was in the hospital. They said it was something with his stomach, that he'd had unbearable pains and his dad convinced his friend Roman to drag him to the emergency room, where they gave him great quantities of morphine. He was out only the one day; the next day he was back, drinking flavored water instead of the four or five Cokes he habitually downs during the shift. On the third day he had returned to his usual pace. I saw him in the back talking to Pablo.

Our ladder-back chairs have a decorative hole in the top rung, and late one afternoon I came around the corner of the bar and saw he'd stuck his cock through the hole there. Just to shock me or anyone else who walked by. Somehow he knows which girls can handle this and which can't.

Other guys imitate him sometimes. Once Casey told me that he let his dick hang out underneath his apron all night, and because he's about six-three, when he was standing at his tables his junk would rest on the tabletop, hidden behind the apron. Then last Sunday I was in the office before the shift started, talking to Rich, the maître d'. Kansas John walked in to ask me if he could pay me to do his alcohol seller-server recertification for him. I said yes, so he was writing down his information for me, and behind his back Rich unzipped his pants and pulled it out. He wadded it up in his hand and waited for Kansas John to turn around. But before Kansas turned around, Anna walked in the door of the office. I don't know how Rich did it fast enough, but he covered it with his hands as if he just had his hands in his lap.

Danny and his roommate like to have the same women. Lou Ambrogetti is the Cuban-Italian chef at Il Castello. He is short, bronze, and beautiful, and though he's only thirty-four, the stubble atop his round head is pigeon-colored. His full lips hold still underneath a gaze that's pruriently curious, and a tattooed sun circumscribes his navel. One Saturday night I sucked him off at the bottom of the back stairs behind Cosimo, the nightclub affiliated with our restaurant. I was there only because one of the owners, Mr. Salvatore

Lissandri, brought me over from the steakhouse in his Aston Martin; it was Sal himself who'd given me a job at The Restaurant.

———

Lissandri philandered. But first—he came into the Dream Café, one of the two restaurants I was working in that year, a few mornings a week for breakfast. We fought over him, whoever else was on the breakfast shift and I, because he always tipped $15, which worked out to be one hundred sixty percent of his $9 tab. He ate steel-cut organic oatmeal with no brown sugar and soy milk on the side, followed by four egg whites scrambled with spinach and tomatoes. He drank water only, with a straw. He didn't say much to us and always had the paper with him. A native New Yorker and Mets fan, he stared at the sports section while he did business on his mobile phone all during his breakfast.

When Jamie started waiting on him he put the phone down. She was new, a yoga instructor from Woodstock, in town to save money by living with her folks so she could take a trip to India to develop her practice. Sal liked her—we all did, she radiated bliss and vigor. He flirted with her and told her she ought to come over to his restaurant, he'd set her up in the bar over there. She turned him down because she didn't want to work nights.

One Sunday Sal came in with his sometime companion, Laura, at the peak of brunch service. The Dream Café was not a well-run restaurant and as the strongest server I often took six or seven tables at once. From ten a.m. till about one in the afternoon I'd feel like I was continuously on the pre-

carious edge of a sheer food-service cliff. What heroics I performed to get people their fucking brunch. Sal and Laura sat
down on the patio that morning—I had never seen him in on
the weekend, or even during the volume part of any weekday. I already had a half dozen booths in the lanai going, but
as I flew past them he said Can you take care of us here? I
said Absolutely. I rang in his food and miraculously it was on
the table five minutes later. That day he left me $20, a raise.

The following Tuesday I woke up and knew he'd be
coming in. (My daughter and I have this slight ability to
sense things—mostly insignificant things. Once I decided in
the shower to wear this purple shirt—I visualized it and she
heard me somehow. She came to me in the bathroom and
said she wanted to pick out my shirt. I looked into her eyes,
which are the pure glittering blue of a sky far removed from
any inhabited place, and thought about my purple shirt. She
went to my closet and I followed. She reached up above her
head and grabbed its sleeve.)

That morning I woke up in my shithole apartment in the
warren of Latino complexes near Park Lane and Greenville
Avenue. Black mold on one wall and in six months I had
never cooked a meal there because it would have seemed de
facto contaminated. I woke up and knew Sal would be coming in, so with my Dream Café T-shirt I put on some makeup
and my grandmother's lapis bead necklace. I didn't usually
bother with makeup at six a.m., but I wanted a different life.
I wanted to ask him soon, before the memory of my Sunday
service dissipated.

When I dropped the check I said I have a question
for you.

Okay, he said, and sat back. I said I was wondering if you had any openings in your restaurant. He said Sure, I'll hire you. Come in on Friday, I'll tell Danny to get you going.

Easy as that.

———

So after I had been there a month I guess he decided he wanted to try me out, and on a Saturday night he put his hand on my elbow and said I heard you were gonna buy me a drink at Cosimo. I said Oh? He said Come with me. I told the closing manager that Sal wanted me to go with him, and I was abruptly granted amnesty from sidework, which didn't exactly do much for my standing with the rest of the waitstaff. I got into Sal's car and he told me I had to take off my vest and tie before we went in, so I left them on the white leather seat, along with my phone. At the club he schmoozed Dallas's most expensive, meticulously produced women, periodically coming back over to bump against me in my dirty dark gray button-down work shirt. When the lights went up at last call, he was gone, my phone and uniform with him. I don't know if he ditched me because he found something better—likely—or because he saw me with Lou—also likely. That was several weeks before I ended up at his palatial Highland Park house.

While he was stroking the glamorous ones I was meeting Lou. He opened his fly in the middle of the dance floor and let his penis hang out underneath his shirt, which concealed it, though not completely. It was an interview. It was a question about me, which I answered by grabbing it. The music thrummed so loudly he had to say in my ear What are you doing later? I said What are you doing now?

We went out the back door and down the stairs. At the bottom of the stairs he held his beer in one hand and took mine with the other. I went down on him and got him off before two minutes had passed. We went back upstairs and he told me his phone number, which I remembered and borrowed a phone to call when I found myself stranded at two a.m.

I took a cab to his and Danny's condo. Inside we did lines and fucked. Ambrogetti is the only guy I know who can fuck on coke. Everybody else it makes limp. The worst is, they're horny and limp. They want you to work hard on it but it never responds. I stayed up all night with Lou and Danny and two other guys who took turns with me.

And so on. In about three months' time I had sex with approximately thirty different men who worked for or patronized my steakhouse, the bar next door, Il Castello, and Cosimo. Three managers, one owner, two sous-chefs, one busser, one bartender, a dozen servers and as many customers, the latter group including Danny's father and a preponderance of surgeons and athletes. They began to say about me She don't play and She's for real. Once I was turning in my cashout, getting ready to leave for the night, and a server I hadn't yet been with asked me if he could buy me a beer next door. I said Do you want to fuck? He chuckled, taken aback, and said No, I just want to buy you a beer. You know, hang out and talk and stuff, that's all. I said Oh. No, that's okay. Thanks, though. In the days afterward I heard this story repeated while people were folding napkins or polishing silverware, and it became a totemic tale about me that people distributed to new servers.

Calvin was my confessor—every afternoon I'd tell him about the new ones and spare no detail, be it of ugliness or danger. He would call me out, question my judgment, show me a worry I wanted to feel for myself. I didn't hide from Calvin how much I pretended. Pretended to like it, pretended to want it, pretended to have orgasms. He didn't understand and I couldn't explain. It had something to do with love and something to do with grief. It was just this: I'd be down on the floor sometimes, picking up fallen chunks of crab cake near some diamond broker's shoe, with my apron and my crumber and my *Yes, sir, certainly, right away,* and I'd feel impaled by the sight and feel of the half-eaten crabmeat because it wasn't her sparkly laugh and it wasn't that place on her shoulder, right up against her neck, that smells like sunlight. *I am not a mother,* I'd think as I walked to the trash can. You can fuck a lot of people, Calvin would say to me, and still enjoy yourself. Make it about you, about pleasure. At least make it safe. But it wasn't about pleasure; it was about how some kinds of pain make fine antidotes to others. So when they gave me their numbers and they were old and I'd seen them with hookers, I said yes.

And so on. There was the night with Casey and Florida John. They got me high and then played Call of Duty while taking turns with me. I stayed in the bedroom on the bed. I would do a line and then a bong hit and one of them would fuck me. Then that one would go back out to the living room to play and I would do another line and another bong hit while I waited for the other one. I don't know how many times this repeated.

There was the night with Casey and Howard, and the night with Greg and Howard, and the night with Greg and Casey. There was the night I sat next to Greg on the sidewalk outside his apartment while he talked to his girlfriend on the phone. What are you wearing? he asked her. Then we went inside and I got down on the floor in a sandwich between him and Gray. I faced Greg because I didn't want to look at Gray, who was small and dour. Gray ground on me while Greg fucked me. Greg came fast and then Gray pushed into me but there was no rhythm or confidence in his motions and he couldn't climax. Greg laughed. Come on, Gray, you can do it, man! Let's take a break, I said to Gray. I went into the living room to find drugs or a drink. Someone who looked like a full-size, better, happier version of Gray was sitting on the couch. Who are you? I asked. I'm Gray's brother Blake, he said. He didn't say anything about whatever he had heard from the other room. Hey will you help me get on that thing? he asked me, pointing to an inversion table in the corner of the room. If I can have the rest of that, I said, holding my hand out for his drink. He gave it to me and I drank it. It was a screwdriver. We went to the inversion table and got him strapped in. I wasn't much help. Then he closed his eyes and flipped it and he was hanging upside down in front of me. He was wearing sweatpants. I knelt in front of him and grabbed the waistbands of his sweatpants and his boxers and pulled them away from his body and up over his cock. Whoa! he said. What are you doing? I don't know, I said, I've never done this before. Then I sucked on him and he said Okay, you can do that. His pelvis was directly level with my mouth. When I felt him getting close I put my hands on either side of the table and rocked it back and forth. It was a lot easier on my neck that way. Behind the table I saw Gray come into the room and stand there watching us. When Blake started to orgasm I saw Gray leave.

The next time Gray and I were on the same shift was a few days later. He came up to me by the lockers and said Hey I'm sorry about the other night, that I didn't—you know. He said it like it must have offended me. I was embarrassed for him, that he had been thinking about it. It's fine, I said. No big deal.

There was the Cajun sous-chef I spent two or three nights with, who told me his fiancée had hung herself. He pointed to one of the rafters in his loft. Later we had an intern from the local culinary school—I think she was only eighteen. They started her on the dessert line with the Cajun sous-chef training her, and I watched him macking on her hard and I watched her buy it. She got pregnant and they fired the Cajun sous-chef and hired a new sous-chef who was part Inuit. His name was Reggie but everyone called him Eskimo. He even had Eskimo embroidered on his chef's coat. One night I went to the Westin downtown with Eskimo. It was his suggestion and I'm not sure why he didn't want to go back to his house, but I didn't want to go back to my house either. He didn't have money for the hotel room though so I paid for it. I took a long shower hoping he would fall asleep while I was in the bathroom but he didn't. He was really heavy and graceless. When the culinary intern, who had continued to work at The Restaurant after the Cajun sous-chef was fired, had her baby they hired a Salvadoran woman to do desserts. I watched Eskimo train her, putting his hands on hers to show her how to pipe the whipped cream onto the cheesecake. She had a daughter the same age as mine, and she always said How's your niña? when she saw me. Eskimo got her pregnant—no lie. They didn't fire him. Maybe they were afraid if they fired him it would just happen again with the next sous-chef. The Salvadoran woman had the baby and married Eskimo, and when she left The Restaurant to stay home with her baby they hired a man for the dessert line. Everyone told him to be careful not to get pregnant back there.

One rainy night in April Danny took me into the office—he had to kick another manager out with a look—and bent me over the desk. My head knocked the phone off its cradle. He said I think Lou's waiting for you in The Private Room. I went into The Private Room and Lou bent me over. Lou went back to his date in the bar, and later she was so drunk she let him fuck her at the host stand. All the customers were gone, but Justin and I watched. Andy Vanderveer took a picture with his camera phone. That was one of my highest-grossing shifts, too—while I was getting fucked by the general manager and his best friend I had probably twenty-five covers running in the bar. I think I made around $700 that night. After Lou fucked his date I carried her out to the car. I'm not a big woman—I weigh about 115 pounds and I'm five-five. I was wearing a cocktail dress and heels, but I picked her up in my arms like a baby and put her in the front seat. Her name was Indica, a breed of marijuana plant.

When I'd puff it was so much easier to get down. I used to imagine a small tribe of aborigines living inside me, representative en masse of my true identity, and I always knew they thought me reckless whenever I'd end up in some dark place with some feral soul. I liked to smoke them out, to puff and puff until I got them all up in the hills so I could do whatever I was doing and they'd be unaware. For example, the ex-pro who stood seven feet tall and came into the bar in May. His enormous cock was the size of a rolling pin and not nearly as domesticated. He measured me in the restaurant: when I delivered his salad he said Whyntcha sit here fo a minute and pulled me down on his lap. I guess he judged my ass adequate and we met later at the W, where I slammed the shots he bought me, to demonstrate that I was not afraid of whatever debasement awaited. He noted this and nodded to the bartender for another as he said Like a champ, huh? Baby have one more, it'll help. In the corner of a dark parking lot we lit a blunt for more help. Eventually I felt that haze come between me and the natives, the little people inside, so I was separated from their judgments and they were protected from my actions for a while. He said What's up. You okay? Ready? I'm'onna give it to you. Inside the truck he fucked me in the ass, and his cock took up so much room in me it seemed logistically impossible that he'd done it. Like if you heard a school bus drove into a pup tent.

That could have been the last. After that one I wanted to say to my indigenous selves *This is fine, here's good, this is far enough. We'll camp here for the night and make our ascent in the morning.* But I didn't, and on June eighth at the bar next door Mickey, one of the senior servers, pimped me out. He told me to go outside with his friend James, who didn't work at The Restaurant and whom I'd never seen before. We got into my car and James told me to suck his dick. What reluctance I felt at the sight of his slack penis flopped over on his thigh. (By that time the natives didn't linger. They just slipped out the back of me quick and let the fire door slam.) When it got hard he wanted to fuck, so I got in the passenger seat underneath him. There were servers and kitchen guys in the parking lot drinking after work and I'm sure they all saw the car rocking. I was thinking it might be over soon when the passenger door opened and Mickey stood there, watching his friend fuck me. He got right down in my face and poured a Modelo Especial all over my head and neck. He said That's right you like it you're such a slut. He's fucking you good isn't he. I said Shut the door, Mickey, and wiped beer out of my eyes while James continued to fuck as if he were oblivious. Mickey slapped my cheek and said Shut up shut the fuck up. I said Okay and stared at him impassively. James fucked. Mickey opened the back door of the car so he could reach me better because the seat was reclined. He poured beer on me and hit my face and called me a bitch and hit my face, and I thought about her sleeping in her dad's living room half an hour away. I wondered which pajamas she was wearing and if he had found her missing favorite stuffed fox yet. After James got out of me and out of the car I quit using drugs and started parking in front of the restaurant so that when my shift was over I wouldn't have to walk past anyone who might offer me a beer, a drag, or a bump, or tell me they wanted their duck sicked.

———

Yesterday Danny walked through the mother station—what we call the area in the back where we make tea and

coffee and prep bread baskets—singing *Fuckin shiiiiiiiit,
fuckin shiiiiiiiiit* to the tune of the *Rocky* theme. He went
into the employee bathroom, where he shaves every day
before service while conferring with one or the other of his
inner circle. When he came out he said, as he adjusted his tie,
Fuckin suck my balls, bitches. I'm starvin.

He strides lankily through the main dining room
around five p.m. every day, half-dressed in his suit trousers
and a Yankees T-shirt. He sees everything. He can tell if
you're chewing gum from all the way across the cavernous
dining room, which we keep so dark we have to give the
guests flashlights to read the menu. He hates it when you
don't make sure there's enough room to work around your
tables—at the height of dinner service sometimes you have
only six inches of space between chair backs, and the path
from the kitchen line to the farthest tables becomes labyrin-
thine if not unnavigable. Danny will walk past your five-top
and say Sister-love, would you please scoot this fucker a cunt
hair to the right so we don't dump mac 'n' cheese all over the
fat-ass in seat two?

Miguel Loera will be sending out the mac 'n' cheese
when dinner service starts, but right now he's talking to one
of the other servers about Chivas, the fútbol team favored
and followed by most of our kitchen staff. Miguel runs the
kitchen line for Chef. He is a magician, he never fucks up.
He calls me Maestra, because I sometimes wear lentes that
make me look bookish. I call him Miguelito or Maestro. He
always leaves the second button on his chef's coat unbuttoned, for luck. When I first see him in the afternoon as I

walk past the kitchen I'll catch his eye and pat my heart, where that button rests on his coat, in a gesture of solidarity. Yesterday he asked me if I had a good time with my family for Easter. Did you find eggs? he asked. You kid look for the little huevos? I said, Yes, we looked for little huevos. Did you look for eggs? I asked. No, he said, I no look. Ah, I said, but did someone look for your little huevos? Yes, he said with a grin, someone find my little huevos and they eat them.

When he calls me to run food he always says Maestra, don't hate me, you take one mash and one mush to twenty-three please. Or Maestra, ¿sabes que te amo, verdad? I do anything for you, just do this one poquito thing for me please. Sometimes he sneaks me a crab cocktail at the end of the night because he knows I love it, the tender jumbo lump crabmeat lightly dressed with lemon and parsley, a bit of cocktail sauce on the side.

Often the Mexicans ask me if I am enojada, or ¿Por qué estás triste, Mari? they wonder. ¿Que te molesta, Mari-quita? It's because I'm perpetually lost in thought and wear a sunken, anxious face. I say No, I'm not mad. I'm not sad either. Nothing's bothering me. Miguel asks me Maestra, what are you thinking about? He doesn't love you anymore? I say He never loved me, he just fucks me. Miguel tells me that last year the woman he loved was pregnant with twins, his first children. For reasons no sabemos she decided to have an abortion and she left him. He tells me he couldn't work, he would cry while he was running the line every day, every night he would get so drunk. He kept trying to quit but Danny wouldn't let him. He says to me And now, Maestra,

I'm fine. See? Look at me. I want to die then. But now—what can you do? Stop thinking about it, thinking is no good for you. I say Okay, Maestro, claro. No más thinking.

He's right, it's important to buck up every night and breathe deeply and be happy for the people so they'll want to believe you when you call the $140 Kobe filet the best beef in the world and promise it will actually melt in their mouths. You have to stay bright to get them on a bottle of Caymus or Cakebread, you can't be lurking in the back of your melancholy head. Sometimes I think this is why Danny says Suck my balls whenever I walk past him—it's spoken with the utmost affection and the utmost defiance. When he says Suck it he's saying It's a circus, honey-love, so fuck those motherfuckers. And when my retort is Get it out I'm saying Here we are being hard and relentlessly dazzling in spite of whatever shit. We are saying to each other If you have an affliction, any remorse or anguish, eat it, drink it, snort it, fuck it, use it, suck it, kill it.

I work five shifts and I pay for your after-school care and your health insurance and I give your dad a third of the money I make. He brings you by the restaurant each Friday, because I have to come in to pick up my tips for the week and it's closer to him than my apartment. Plus you like it, and I like showing you off. You're just old enough to know we've been through something and young enough to not hold it against me. Your dad drives through the porte cochere around dusk, before many guests have arrived, and you get a kick out of how the valets open your door and call you ma'am. I wait for you in the lobby, enjoying the luxuries of sitting and street clothes. The maître d' greets you with Good evening, miss, and a peppermint and you run to me.

One Friday Cal intercepts you, asking you where you're going so fast, like you're in trouble. When Cal is giving you all his mischievous attention like that you feel like you're the one. To my mama, you say, laughing. No you stay with me, Cal says, stay with me until you tell me where you got those blue eyes. From God, you say. That's right, Cal says, and then to me, You been takin this child to church? No sir, I say, it wasn't me. Well Miss Mamalisa is it that time? Cal asks you. *Ana*-lisa, you laugh. That's what I said, he says, is it time, Mamalisa? *Ana*-lisa! you say, not laughing. That's what I said! You got a hearing problem? He looks at me. Have you had her ears checked? I think it's yours that are malfunctioning, I say to Cal, and I can tell you are happy I am on your side. What do you mean, says Cal, I'm just asking Mamalisa here if it's Shirley Temple time or not! Mama, make him stop, you say to me, scrambling around Cal to come sit with me. I can't make him do anything, I say, he does what he wants. I don't like it when he calls me Mama, you say. She doesn't like it when you call her Mama, I say to Cal. Okay ladies, Ana, I'm sorry, Marie, I apologize, shall we step into the bar? he says, offering us his arms. Ana, can I call your mama Mama? Is that okay with you? he asks you. Yes, you say, Mama's Mama.

————

We go out to dinner at La Calle Doce with a friend who says you make him think of the song Jolene. You color a sombrero and eat chips and bar garnishes—orange wedges, maraschino cherries, cucumber slices. You color maracas. My friend buys a song from the mariachis for you. Don Gato: You follow the story as if it is the most important news, and when Don Gato comes back to life at the end your relief is immense.

There is a wishing well in the middle of the dining room, a koi pond lit amber. You ask for a penny and then you sit on the low mosaic tile wall through three entire courses while we talk. After dessert I come to collect you, thinking you have been mesmerized by so many iridescent fish all this time. But your face is troubled. What's wrong? I say.

Mama, you say, I don't know what to wish for.

You give me the sweaty penny and say You can have my wish.

Thank you, I say. That's thoughtful.

I think, my arm around your waist. I close my eyes for effect and I see The Restaurant. I see the way Casey stands when he takes an order at a table. I hear Asami's beautiful laugh. I'm so glad that in this one exact moment I'm not waiting tables, not locked into that place across town for the night. But I still feel it going on. It's always there. I flick the coin into the water and open my eyes. We watch it flutter to the bottom, and then we go home.

The Dangler

Shaila has a body to break your mind. You scan it once expecting a flaw, twice not believing there isn't one, three times for the exhilaration. The way her legs are tan, a real brown sugar tan, her calves all cut up and high, her toes manicured but in that simple nude style, her ass so round, so beautiful. Her slender waist, her perfect all-real breasts floating and pulling the world to her, nipples often showing—just a bit, if she turns—through whatever silk dress she's wearing. She has long straight dirty blond hair that falls over her face when she checks her phone. She's gorgeous but in a porchy Alabama way, not the way women in Dallas usually look if they're trying. Like you look at her and think that must be about how she looked before she went into her big bathroom to get ready.

I'm good enough to get the once-over in the bar at The Restaurant, I see them thinking my smallness is appealing, my ass and face are cute enough, I see them thinking that short haircut might be sexy. I'm always in a backless cocktail dress and heels, I'm flat chested and a tad muscular so they ask me if I'm a dancer and say Call me sometime, let's have a drink. It took me a while to understand you're supposed to work that for your money but you can let the willingness fall right off your face when you turn around. It took me a while to understand that of course men fling their entreaties out in swarms, like schools of sperm, hoping one will stick. They're expecting to be turned down so you shouldn't feel any obligation.

I've seen every woman in Dallas bring her best into the bar but Shaila's the one who stops time and mouths. She's easy like a man too which makes them insane. God she's dirty, they slobber. They're all after her and she gives them all their turns, letting them outspend each other. Ahmed owns a pizza company that runs catchy snarky ads, he's a Pakistani New Yorker who knows Danny from the Bronx. He left his wife and four kids for Shaila but now he sits at the corner of the bar all sad and blurred, staring into the middle whiskey distance.

Frank, one of my regulars, told me she fucks like a spider monkey, whatever that means. He took her to the Bahamas. Danny took her to Vegas and they got so blown out in the hotel room they couldn't make their dinner time at Pagliacci, when that was a reservation a normal person couldn't get in a lifetime of trying. She used to be married to the guy who started Glamorous You, a multimillion-dollar mall make-over photography company, so she made out like a king in the divorce and she can just hang out in the bar every night or take off for the Bahamas.

She drives an orange Ferrari. I heard it's the only one that color. They call her the Dangler because once she came to the bar when it was that time and she was wearing a black dress the size of an eyelash. I guess she sat on the barstool some way and somebody saw the string. I guess if you have all that money and that body it doesn't matter what people call you.

Best pussy of my life, Frank told me, it's all over after the Dangler.

———

There's this other woman I call the other dangler in my head. I was waiting behind her at the Public Storage to get a spot to store his TV and his records and that green chair because I didn't have room for them in my new place. I don't know why I did that for him, I even paid for the storage. Had to borrow a truck and call up my ex because the only truck I could borrow was a stick and I can't drive a stick.

Some advice: Don't call your ex to help you do anything for your current hateful man who's in Miami for the summer probably making some memories, at least not if the last time you were sitting in that green chair watching that TV the hateful man said, about you, This is the best pussy I can get right now.

So the woman in front of me was jammed up about something at the Public Storage, while my ex was waiting outside with the truck.

I can't do that, she kept saying, you don't understand. She'll kill me. I need to handle this while she's away. I've been in the hospital. I'm supposed to be there now I just got to handle this.

She had seaweedy hair divided into two ponytails,

the bands had those pink plastic balls. She was wearing a Mickey Mouse T-shirt and stonewashed denim cargo shorts. She was skinny in an unhealthy way and her toenails were yellow and clawy in some of those black rubber sandals with all the straps, like feet tires. I didn't ever see her face, just stood behind her while she tried to get something from the Public Storage woman. From her elbow skin I'd guess early forties. But maybe younger factoring in hard living. She had a purse with a Mickey Mouse keychain hanging off it and her keys were clipped to her belt with a Mickey Mouse carabiner. She had an anklet on each ankle, a Mickey Mouse charm dangled from each one. Finally she yelled at the Public Storage woman.

Ughhh! You do not understand, she will freaking kill me. I just need to put this in there like she said. She's waiting for me right outside, why does she have to come in?

I thought you said she was away, the Public Storage woman said coldly.

I turned around with my arms crossed in front of me like I just wanted a change of scenery but I was really looking to see if there was somebody out there. I saw my ex, who gave me a high sign like What the fuck is taking so long, and in the parking spot right past him was a bigger truck, a white Chevy Silverado. There was a woman in the driver's seat, she looked about fifty and she had long white hair that she smoothed back with a hand that had a ring on each finger. She was nodding her head and slapping her knee to some music. The other dangler gave up arguing and said as she went out the door God! People don't got to be so damned ugly! Her Mickey Mouse carabiner caught on the handle, jerking her back. The bell on the door jangled roughly as she worked the carabiner off the handle. Outside, she climbed into the bed of the truck and the driver started backing out before she'd even sat down on the toolbox, making her lose her balance. She yelled at the driver and banged on the window behind the gun rack. The driver didn't turn around, just kept nodding her head to the music.

————

Frank said the spider monkey thing to me one day when I was running some errands for him. He was a criminal lawyer who did a lot of big white-collar cases and handled all the minor shit for his friends—Danny's traffic tickets, the bar's occasional health code violations, the DUI Ahmed got after Shaila dumped him to go to Cabo with Matt, this personal trainer who had stopped drinking alcohol but still came to the bar three nights a week to get coke from Danny. He'd down glass after glass of iced tea, usually in one draw. You'd refill the glass and he'd be doing his little Splenda ritual, shake shake tear pour stir—and when you turned around again the glass would be empty.

He was the one who had it worst for Shaila, even worse than Ahmed. You could tell by how they sat at the table— she'd be leaning back giving off this all-balls safari-guide vibe and Matt would sit forward in his chair to catch the invisible gazelles of wisdom leaping out of her mouth. He was a nervous tense one with those gigantic biceps not good for anything but reps. Probably the only thing whiter than the pure coke Danny got him and made him pay out his demolished septum for was his teeth, which glowed ultraviolet in the bar. He laughed at everything Shaila said and leaned forward more and drank more tea and went to the bathroom to snort more off the key to his Avalanche, which he didn't valet, because he wanted to keep his keys or because he wasn't loaded like Shaila's other fuckems I don't know. Eventually he'd come back from his latest trip to the men's room chewing the invisible gum.

So I did these runarounds for Frank, who had a receptionist and a legal secretary and a junior attorney but still needed someone to handle things like his lunch and shoes for the women he was seeing. He told me he'd been having drinks with Danny and Ahmed at Trece one night when Danny got a text from Shaila. It said *what time can I fit you in tonight my love?* and Danny was showing it to Frank saying I fucking love this whore she's such a fine dirtleg always ready when Frank got a text from Shaila: *what time can I fit you in tonight my love?* Frank was pissed she texted Danny first and Danny was about to go public with his alpha male stock when Ahmed said You cocksuckers it's just D before F. I got it first. She don't give a fuck about any of us.

That's what's so great about her, said Frank, and Danny said What do you want Ahmed? Christ. Sweet cunt, no bullshit.

————

That is what I've tried to give my hateful man but it hasn't worked out. My hateful man is Ghanaian British and tall and mean and has a gift for hats. The selection of, and the wearing of in such a way as to crack my dumb heart. He plays jazz trombone for a twelve-piece that's going places and he's proud of the strong embouchure and extra-muscular tongue he brings me. In bed only is he sweet and sometimes when his fluttering lick releases me I almost cry with the ache for him to be that gentle in the hallway, or the living room. But he's brushed me back one too many times for me to let him see how much I want that. He doesn't like for me to sit next to him on the couch, or any nonfucking touching in general, but he'll tickle me sometimes. He had me pinned to the floor one night and he wouldn't stop even though I was seriously asking him to and I was a little drunk so I spit on him because I couldn't move anything else. Suddenly he was very still and he wiped the spit off his face with his right hand. He was a little drunk too and as I was sitting up he hit me across the face with the spit hand so hard my head slammed back into the green chair. Fuck! he said, looking at his hand. It was his slide hand and he had a show the next night.

To apologize for anything he'd put on a record and share his enthusiasm with me. As if to say Nothing can be all that bad if we're enjoying this brilliance together. That night it was Coleman Hawkins' high hopeful "Body & Soul", the sax's silky tremble more human than a voice. My hateful man also made incredible tacos for me no matter how late it was when I got out of work. These may seem like nothing, but even if you yourself can tell how paltry the spread is it's yours so it glitters and you don't want to turn away from it.

My ex punched the wall the one time he wanted to hit me, and I probably deserved it. He had this striking autumn-red beard and warm brown eyes and wanted only to make me happy but I would yell at him for buying the wrong orange juice etc. He would have done anything for me, he even gave me an enema once when I had a strange disease that had compacted my shit so hard I went to the ER. He never minded getting up when the baby cried in the middle of the night and he would change her and bring her back to me. But I slept with everyone at work so he put his fist through the sheetrock and we broke up. He plays guitar at night when he gets home, and he teaches special ed at the middle school. That's the sort of guy he is.

I wish I didn't want the exotic man who knows the entire history of jazz, and instead wanted the teacher, who has his flaws but whose kindness is as rare as genius.

———

Frank had me pick up a necklace for the Dangler from this Arab jeweler who owed him. It was a custom-made pendant—a tiny white gold spider with a heart-shaped sapphire on its back. She'd been wearing this choker made of rubies and black pearls that Matt bought her in Cabo, he must have remortgaged his condo for that thing. Frank had me write the note to put in the box with the sapphire spider: *To the Dangler, the player with the heart of cold. Dangle this. XO Frank.*

I saw the other dangler again when I was on my way to get Frank's sandwich and drop off the necklace. Shaila lived in a penthouse on Turtle Creek and I was supposed to put the gift directly into her hands. As I headed up the freeway I looked to my right and there was the white Silverado. The other dangler was in the back again, one hand gripping the side of the bed, her scrawny forearm tendons popping out.

The other hand was alternately holding the Mickey Mouse keychained purse close to her and moving strings of hair out of her eyes when the wind lashed her ponytails across her face. She was grimacing—smiling?—and the driver was drumming her ringed fingers on the steering wheel, nodding her head in time.

———

Frank had called Shaila's doorman—he had box seats on the fifty at Texas Stadium he used for leverage if people didn't need legal tricks—so the doorman keyed the elevator to the penthouse as soon as I got there. Shaila answered the door in a wife-beater—no bra—and cutoff jeans shorts. She could have put on some heels and come into our five-star joint and no one would have said a thing but What're you having, sister. Her body was like an outfit she never took off. I suddenly felt like I needed a haircut and wished I wasn't wearing sneakers.

Hey, she said.

Two small kids appeared behind her, a girl and a boy. Kids, I thought, Shaila has fucking kids!

They never told me you had kids, I said like an idiot.

Yeah I bet they told you everything else though, she said, but not like she resented it or like she was boasting. It was more a comment on Frank and Danny and Ahmed and how she knew them, knew everything they could possibly think of to do or say.

She turned and hollered Maria! into the penthouse. Go play with Maria, she said to the kids. They ran off.

What can I do for you? she said.

This is from Frank and I was told to put it right in your hands, I said.

Okay, tell him it's the most beautiful thing anybody ever gave me and I want to suck his huge cock until he dies of coming, she said, shoving the black velvet box into one back pocket of her shorts and pulling her buzzing phone out of the other. Hey sexy, she answered, mouthing Thanks to me with one of those all-expenses-paid smiles as she shut the door.

Did you give it to her? Does she like it? Frank texted me. *She LOVES it,* I sent back. Then I figured I should tell him exactly what she said in case she said Did she tell you what I said? later. A woman like Shaila might seem flip and shallow but you could see that she could get you fired if the wrong look crossed her face and the wrong man happened to notice.

Shaila must have really liked the spider though because she started wearing it all the time instead of the choker Matt gave her. Then Matt started drinking again, vodka Red Bulls, he'd drink double talls until he was out of his mind. One night he swung at Danny in the bar but Danny is an Italian street rat and Matt is just a gym rat so Danny ducked and broke his half-full bottle of Heineken on Matt's jaw like he'd seen the punch coming for eight years. Danny's friend Kole was in the bar that night—Kole was a freelance bodyguard who used to be an offensive tackle for the Broncos and was three times the size of Matt. Kole threw him out of the bar and two twenty-bags fell out of Matt's pocket into the pool of beer on the floor as Kole was relocating him. Jesus, Kole! Shaila said from her barstool, Don't fucking kill him!

He's a big boy, he be all right, said Kole. You're a much bigger boy, she said, searching for the straw of her mojito without taking her eyes off him.

Danny picked up the twenty-bags and shook them off and told me to get Niño to clean up that stupid queer fuckwad's mess. He bought all the customers in the bar a shot to make nice and then he and Shaila left in the orange Ferrari.

———

The next day when I got to work Ahmed was already on his stool.

Did you hear? he said.

We used to chat when he'd wait for Shaila, she'd made him so happy he was extra-friendly with everyone, and he palmed me a bill for no reason once. But he hadn't wanted to talk since she dropped him, so the energy in his voice surprised me.

No, I said, what?

That sad fuck Matt ran off the bridge last night, he said. Went right through the construction barrier and hit a guy. Killed him. Can you believe that? Dumb fuck walked away, too. Broken wrist, that's it. I know it's all that bitch's fault. He lost his shit over her.

Ahmed seemed stunned by this event and also perplexed in a jaded way, as if he couldn't get why it was the next guy over who'd won the disaster lottery. As if he wished he could have been the one to blow up his life because of Shaila.

Later that week I heard that Frank was leaning on the prosecutor to get him to drop the DWI since Matt was already up for manslaughter. And Danny became Shaila's consoler, when she came into the bar he had her drink ready and he sat with her all night long, his arm around her. He tried to make her laugh in a special sensitive way that acknowledged she didn't want to. When she wasn't in the bar I heard him playing family therapist on his cell phone, pacing in the lobby:

It's not your fault. You didn't make him do it. He wasn't a stable person. You were just having a good time and he couldn't handle it. You didn't do anything wrong, he said, you didn't do anything a man wouldn't do.

One night he hung up after one of these conversations and said I'm taking her to Baja. I'm gonna fuck her brains out, try and take her mind off it.

I slept with Matt, when I was on my streak. It was just once but now I keep seeing the ceiling fan in his room. I stared at it while he was going down on me, thinking of how to ask him to be softer. He was so vigorous about it, the same way he stirred his tea, as if delicacy must be avoided above all.

———

After all that Kole and Shaila became a thing but Frank and Danny would still drink with them in the bar. Danny told me Kole called Shaila Boo and Shaila called Kole's dick Baby Bear.

I won't ask how you know that, I said.

Good honey, he said, then I won't tell you I passed out on the floor of her penthouse and they forgot I was there.

The hateful man was supposed to come back from Miami soon and was sweet-talking me for a smooth reentry but after everything that happened over the summer I wasn't interested. I called him and left a message saying he needed to start paying the rent on the storage space for his stuff. I know none of that shit with the Dangler and the other dangler even happened to me but somehow just watching it made me want to kill whatever yearning self I had inside me. Whatever was in me hoping for something from someone, hanging on.

I was with the hateful man when you got sick. Later I found out it was just a bad cold. But when you are five and you are sick all you want is for your mother to hold you and rock you and I was with him and I didn't answer the phone when your dad called. He left a message saying you were sick and he needed me to take care of you so he could go to work tomorrow but I didn't call him back. The hateful man showed me some pictures of Rome and asked if I thought they were any good. I didn't like them—some trees, some stone. No heart. I drank bourbon with him until it would have been a bad idea for me to drive to you to hold you and rock you. The man fucked me and told me I was drunk like it was a weakness. But his apartment was full of empty bottles. In the morning he drove me home and when he parked in front of my place he said I think I need to fuck you again. As we walked in the door my home phone was ringing. I unplugged the cord. I knelt in front of my loveseat and he got behind me. As he was thrusting he shifted his balance and I tried to adjust to match his position but we went opposite ways and he jammed into me wrong. Fuck! he yelled and doubled over, holding his nuts. You broke my cock! he said. You moved, I said. I'm sorry.

I should have known you'd trip out if I didn't make you wait for it, he said. He winced, lying curled up on my floor with his pants half-down. He spent the next ten days icing his balls and blaming me and muttering about how he should have known better.

I'm sorry, I said again, and I put on my clothes. All I could think about was you, feverish, hurting, wanting me.

———

I acquired a reputation as straitlaced in The Restaurant when I started seeing the hateful man. My colleagues interpreted it as some kind of new leaf or intentional maturity that I never went out with them after work anymore. But it was just that I didn't need that scene to fuck with myself because he did it for me. As the employee roster at The Restaurant was infiltrated by more and more people who didn't know anything about me, and those who did moved on, quit, or were fired, who I was to everyone morphed into this paragon of good work, consistency, professionalism. An example. I ignored new people until they had lasted for three or four months. I came in at five, rocked my shift the same hard way I did every night, no matter how busy or not, and walked out whenever it was over without looking back. I never left without polishing my tables. Not once. There were many nights when I was so exhausted I'd forget which position I had started at, and have to polish the whole thing again just to be safe. No matter how weary I was though I loved the strangeness of the place when it was empty. That every night we could walk onto a blank stage and invent all that. Take The Restaurant from pristine and silent down to a staggering state of chaotic, deafening, and excessive disarray, and then put it all back together like no one was ever there.

Roman and the Bishop

You think we party now, it's nothing like it used to be, Danny's telling the liquor rep. We've already closed but the liquor rep has a deal with Danny—he gets a free steak and of course free drinks whenever he wants and we get a good rate on the whiskey. But the good rate wouldn't matter if the liquor didn't move, and it's a shitty whiskey that nobody would request. So Danny has us telling our tables about it, that it's the new Crown Royal, the next classic. Danny knows it's not and he knows we know he knows. He probably even knows we know this all came about because the liquor rep sent Danny some hookers and high-quality coke on his birthday—Danny said that if the coke's good enough the hookers will be too. Danny is telling the liquor rep a story about his best friend Roman, the bartender:

So Roman says Hey honey I'll give you thirty dollas you come out on the boat with us, come on it'll be fun. Thirty dollas, all right? Is that cool? You're so pretty. Come with us. So she's like All right, all right, and he's like Baby you got any friends? Hell, I'll give you fifty bucks. Fifty dollars. Go find some friends and I'll give em all fifty dollars. We got some guys who wanna have some fun. So she gets her friends and they all come out on the boat and I swear these girls were like seventeen, oh my God it was sick. You have not seen females like these and they were down. No rules there, ya know? We're all wasted, totally out of our minds, and Roman, this guy has the smallest motherfucking cock you ever saw in your whole life but that don't stop him—Roman sits down in this chair on the deck and he's like SUCK MY COCK BITCHES!!! SUCK MY COCK!! and these women take his money and suck his itty-bitty cock and he goes like this (Danny flexes his arms WWF style) and he screams FUCKIN SUCK MY COCK!

The liquor rep sees me standing at the corner of the bar and cuts a glance my direction as he sips his whiskey, looking back at Danny as if to tell him There's a girl over there won't she mind your cocksucking stories, but of course Danny has known I was there all along. What are you having, honey? Danny says to me. You wanna try this new asswater Joey got us? Acts like it's sweet as pussy juice. Danny doesn't say anything to address the liquor rep's unspoken query and he doesn't apologize to me either. I have seen and heard things and I have kept secrets, so he doesn't need to, and he doesn't give a fuck what the liquor rep thinks.

I haven't decided whether or not I want to drink with these two when Felipe the barback's barback appears behind me. Pinche puta madre! he curses, holding the last tray of hot clean highballs he needs to put away before he's done for the night. Danny is pissing on the floor behind the bar top, his silver tie loosened and collar unbuttoned. He's already buzzing hard, after three shots of Patrón—the real Patrón in the cabinet, not the shit tequila we pour for the guests from the Patrón bottle on the display shelf.

When Felipe turns right around in the doorway to head back to the dishroom Danny realizes he pissed on a clean floor. Aw, fuck, he says in Felipe's direction, fuck! Fucking Sanchez told me you didn't mop yet! Where the fuck is Sanchez where did that fucker go! SANCHEZ!! YOU'RE FUCKING FIRED AND I'M GONNA HAVE YOU DEPORTED! THEY'RE COMING FOR YOU RIGHT NOW!

He doesn't mean it. If there is an individual in the restaurant for whom Danny would die, it is undoubtedly Sanchez. He is illegal, and his English is not that good, but he is the one. He is the barback and he has that beautiful momentum you see in the best, with his body in constant motion to mix cocktails, pulling the liquors from the well rail without looking, holding a new ticket in his mouth as he shakes a cosmo hard in his right hand and pours an exact six-ounce glass of chardonnay with his left. It's not any horsing around like you see in the movies, with twirling or flipping bottles—it's more of a pure dervishness that has on occasion made a fool of me as I called for a drink that was already sitting up straight right under my face.

Danny likes to tell the story, when Sanchez is not around, of how Sanchez moved up from dishwasher to glass polisher to busser to barback, and of how he thought Sanchez was going to cry the day he told him to put on a vest and tie—the same uniform as the bartenders. Sanchez makes all the drinks

for the bartenders—guests ask for whatever and Roman or
Ethan will spin around and say Sanchez! Gooserocks! Man-
hattanup! Sevenandseven!—and he makes all the drinks for
the servers too. The bartenders will be leaning against the
liquor cabinets behind them, watching the game on the TV,
and Sanchez will be reaching and pivoting and spinning and
pouring like mad. For this he is tipped out by the bartenders
each night, and he also receives a percentage of the servers'
tips. But we all know there is no way they let him make anything close to what the white English-speaking slow-moving
bartenders make. Still he makes so much compared to the
other Mexicans. He brought his family over. He has a baby
he named after Danny, Sergio Daniel Sanchez.

We joke that Roman can't take a piss without Sanchez.
There are the servers who think the joke is funny, they laugh
like it's so entertaining that Roman gets away with it, like
he's just some harmless putzy fuck and the world is a room
aglow with the coziness of ale and the bonding of all people.
But some of us don't think it's fair that Sanchez busts his ass
so Roman can make six figures. On Roman's birthday they
brought in a big cake and we were all waiting for Roman to
show up and blow out his candles. I was standing right next
to Sanchez in front of the cake. Calvin got restless because
he needed to get back to his table of VIPs and he said Sanchez, where the fuck is this guy? You blow em out. Go on,
you do it. Motherfucker make you make all his drinks can't
even get over here to blow out his own damn candles. Sanchez blew out the candles and took a piece of cake into the
bar for Roman.

Roman is married to the most beautiful woman. I

don't know why she isn't famous she's so beautiful. She is
Puerto Rican and has this skin and this lustrous black hair
and this body to smite you, with its fullness here and there
and its slightness here and there. And her smile—there is
a dimple—my God. She is smart. She is trilingual. She is
so kind and funny her union with Roman is a mystery that
thwarts discovery. I thought until I saw his cock that surely
there was a secret there, and there was, but not the one I
expected. Danny showed me Roman's cock in the office one
night—Danny, it is well-known, is endowed on an order to
make you not want to look directly at it. But when Roman
got his white cock I guess it was more of a docking than an
endowment. Danny said Wanna see his cock? and Roman
said I gotta cock the size of a silverback gorilla's, I swear.
Wanna see?

He got it out, I looked, it barely peeped out from the fur.
He zipped up. He said The silverback gorilla has the smallest
cock in the world.

———

I decide I just want to go home so I decline Danny's offer
of a drink and I'm waiting for him to finish talking to the
liquor rep so I can turn in my cashout when Felipe comes
back into the bar pushing the mop in its yellow wheeled
bucket with one hand. He has something in his other hand
that he holds up for Danny to see. They find this allá, he
says, gesturing with a nod toward the dining room. He sets
a digital camera down on the bar top, a fancy SLR with a big
fat telescopic lens. What table? asks Danny. Felipe doesn't
know.

Sanchez, I think you should take some pictures of me, says Danny, unbuckling his belt, since you couldn't remember to say Felipe already mopped before I pissed on the floor. You know how to work this thing?

Sanchez demurs. I can tell he wants to cooperate because he knows he owes Danny for the mistake, but he hears in Danny's voice a mocking tone and sees a threat in the thrust of Danny's jaw and his sidelong look. The restaurant is a cash cow and it's the only one, there's no corporate office anywhere, there's just Danny, so everybody learns quick that loyalty comes before all. After loyalty, which includes trusting that Danny is smarter than you and has already made all the calculations to be made in any given situation, arriving at the best or only possible verdict or at least the one that works his angle the fastest—after loyalty, there's just the guest and saying yes, so you can get this job down fast if you know Danny's in charge and those are his two things. Sanchez has it down, which means he knows he has to play along here if he doesn't want to end up in deeper shit with Danny—the shit hasn't even turned deep yet, in truth, because Danny's not really going to blame Sanchez for the fact that he pissed on the clean floor and made more work for Felipe. But he might blame Sanchez if Sanchez doesn't pretend to take the blame, which now involves taking the camera Danny's holding out to him.

The camera has been in Uganda and Uganda is in the camera. I will understand this later, when by chance I see the pictures in a national magazine. The magazine runs a cover story on a controversial black religious leader—a profile of his rise to prominence and his recent work in Africa. There will be a picture of him outside an orphanage with his arm around the shoulder of a lean young boy. The boy is wearing a golden baseball cap and is barefoot and the Bishop, as they call him even though he's a Protestant minister, is wearing a brightly colored kente shirt.

Calvin waited on the Bishop and his guests earlier. I helped him get their wine started but I never noticed the camera and Calvin left over an hour ago. After he finds out about the camera he will consider quitting The Restaurant even though he has built up his call parties over the past seven years so that he can count on a fat night every night. Recently one of his regulars left him a $3,000 tip on a $900 tab, which none of us could shut up about until the week before Christmas when one of his other regulars left him $5,000 on $500. Even though you know that about $4,500 of it is because that guy gets off on having a handsome, older, immaculately groomed and well-spoken black man wait on him, and even though you know that about $400 of it is because Calvin is a genuinely beautiful and irresistibly charismatic individual, for neither of which amounts could you possibly qualify even though you know that your skill set is as technically proficient as Calvin's, certainly proficient enough to have deserved the remaining standard of $100, you still can't help feeling stunned by the mighty whoosh of air as fortune passes you by.

One of the Bishop's guests tonight, an Ivy League professor, is in town to give a lecture at a local university for Martin Luther King Day. The $5,000 tip is weeks behind us and Calvin and I have not spoken of it. I didn't work the night it happened, and he was off the following day when I heard about it, but when I saw him next I didn't even have to mention it. We just looked at each other and I raised my eyebrows and shook my head like I'm sorry, I can't love you anymore. But we hadn't actually traded words about it until tonight, when we were both at the caviar bar making amuse plates for our tables, after he had just seen the Bishop come in with his handler and the Professor. Calvin was glowing, he was nervous and excited and talking so fast I said What's with you, Cal? Is Kon back?

Konstantin was the guy who dropped the five Gs on him. We see plenty of celebrities in The Restaurant, and I haven't known of a single one he ever went giddy over—in fact the more famous somebody was the more determined Cal was to act like they were nobody special. *Don't go pussy up around em*, he'd say, *then they think you weak and next thing you know you're dropping shit and spilling shit. Oh excuse me sir I'm so sorry I just got so nervous. Naw. Just do your thing, be cool, work em like they anybody else.* He explained that he was buzzed because he had just asked the Bishop if he could take care of them, which is kind of against the code among servers but since they were black I doubted anyone would protest. The Bishop had said yes, certainly, and had introduced Calvin to the Professor, who, Calvin explained to me, was a well-known Black Power figure in the seventies and had continued a long career in the movement. I peeked around the corner to check him out in the lobby and he looked so fly, with the Afro and the powder-blue suit and the broad-collared shirt he wore open to show the gold chains around his neck, that I asked Calvin, Is he for real? Calvin gave me this look like I was in trouble and said, Is *he* for real?! That man is realer than real. That man was real long before you were. Is he for real! Get out of here. Just get on with your little old ignorant self, he said to me in mock disgust, and when I apologized he told me that the honor of waiting on the Professor was worth more to him than any amount of money he'd ever make off a table. I might not have believed him, except that he gave up his next table so he could focus on the Bishop and the Professor. Even when he'd been so in the weeds with call parties and had more covers running than three other servers put together he had never before given up a table.

The handler goes everywhere with the Bishop. In the magazine I will read how he is a right-hand man out of antiquity, a vizier and appointed prophet, in the form of chief accountant and public relations manager. The Bishop is never seen without him. When they come into The Restaurant the handler will take the server aside at the beginning of dinner to explain how everything is to work—questions of the Bishop will be addressed to the handler, the Bishop is never to see the bill, the Bishop's plate must touch the table first on every course. The handler is the Bishop's personal photographer, too, and after everything goes down I can't think how he could have forgotten such a serious-looking camera unless he was as excited as Calvin about the Professor.

Calvin was on such a high when he left and I am buoyed a bit by his infectious joy, but my night wore me down. I waited on the people who typify our clientele, the people who've made work for the Professor all these years. They seemed to be attorneys, and over dessert one of them was advising another in a loud drunk way about case strategy and he said, Listen, Jack, they're like girlfriends—it's best to have backup, you know what I mean? As they were paying out they were trying to decide where to go next and settled on Silver City, to the disappointment of one of the younger ones who had tentatively suggested that he knew some girls they could call, which was shot down by the one called Jack who said Oh, is this a you buy em you break em type deal? Cause if not I'd rather just have my scotch and look at some titties and call it in. We have a long day tomorrow.

They don't know Danny spends so much money and time at Silver City that they could get VIP treatment just by mentioning his name. There are a few male servers who might discreetly apprise Danny of their table's intent to go over there, and if Danny feels like it he might make a call, and then the server could go back and lean over next to the one who paid the bill, the one who said it was best to have backup, and the server might whisper to him that the GM had them all set up over there, and there would be an exchange of Man, you didn't have to do that, and No, it's my pleasure, and Thanks, pal, and Don't mention it, just come back, and Oh we definitely will, and You should ask for me, I'll take care of you and Sure, man, you take care of us we'll take care of you, that's how it works right? And that server would have scored a call party and maybe a little extra in a handshake. I can't do it, I mean I don't want to but it would come off wrong from a girl anyway.

I am tired and I want to go home and take off my boy suit, the vest and the double Windsor-knotted tie and the button-down shirt. I want to take a shower. But you don't interrupt Danny. Even Ana, who's six, knows this, has known it from the first time I brought her up to The Restaurant on payday and Danny shook her hand and looked her in the eye and said How are you tonight ma'am. When she tells me she wants to work in a restaurant when she grows up I don't tell her this wasn't my ambition when I was her age and it still isn't. I just say to myself Don't fuck up. If I don't cross Danny and I don't let any of it get to me the money is so good I can turn it into something else, something honorable.

Sanchez is trying to say that he really has no idea how to work the camera or any camera at all ever, No sé, jefe, no sé, he is repeating with his hands in the air as Danny shouts over him, Don't fuck with me, I know you're fucking fucking with me, Sanchez, don't do it, but the closing valet comes into the bar to drop off the liquor rep's keys because his is the last car in the lot. If he were famous or rich they'd wait around for him but he's like one of us now. The valet's entrance distracts Danny from his harassment of Sanchez. Hey, he says to the valet, I met your sister tonight, we bought her and her friends some appetizers and drinks, I think they had a good time. The valet says Yeah, she's visiting from L.A. so I told her she should come up here and check it out. Thanks for doing that for her. You want me to lock up? he asks.

This is sharp of him, to know that Danny likes to lock the front door after the valets leave, and to offer to do it for him. Danny notices if you go out of your way. The valet is in a bad hurry to get home after such a long night, just like the rest of us, to get to whatever it is he has waiting for him, probably weed or coke, maybe just a beer or a woman, and whatever that thing is it starts to pull on you hard late at night. When your shit is done you jet. Danny has his own habits that must be taken up nightly but not until he has closed the place down, and the valet's gesture lets him stay at the bar and pour himself another shot. He pours one for the valet too and tosses him his keys. Here, he says, holding out the shot, Thanks buddy. Just leave my keys by the office on your way out the back door. Tell your sister come back anytime. They down the tequila and Danny throws his shot glass on the floor where he pissed. It shatters and he turns back to Sanchez.

Fuck it, Sanchez, I'll deal with you later, he says, but he picks the camera up off the bar and slings the strap over his shoulder. I'm goin to Silver City soon as I get this bar drawer counted. Roman's already there. You wanna come? he asks the liquor rep. Now that the valet is gone he starts telling the liquor rep about the valet's sister. You can tell she's got something in her, he says. She's real pretty but she has— you know, her hair's different and shit, so I asked her where she's from. She says Oh I'm from Jersey, and I say, So . . . where are your parents from? And she says, My mom is German and my dad's American. And I say, American! There's no American! What do you mean American? Well, he's from Houston, she says. Houston! I say. So? I'm from New York but that don't mean nothing, I'm *Italian*-American. And finally she says, Well my dad's African-American. Oh! Danny says to the liquor rep, so her dad's black! But she wasn't that pretty, I wouldn't fuck her.

———

Danny has me do various administrative tasks for The Restaurant because he hates the tedious paperwork side of the business, so I'm in the office paying some invoices the next day when he shows up in his street clothes, rather than the $2,000 handmade Italian suits I'm used to seeing on him. His after-hours hip-hop accessorization used to perplex me but I'm starting to get it. If you want to be a gangster you have to look like one. The spotless puffy white sneakers, the hoodie, the huge black tinted-window SUV, the playing of serious games. At all moments he defies you to underestimate him.

The office is an unventilated fire hazard, a closet of a room that has accumulated various computers and filing cabinets and broken-down pieces of The Restaurant like busted chairs and menus whose leather spines have torn. Banker's boxes of outdated cashouts encroach on the safe and the copier so when you want to get paid or reprint the wine list it's like one of those strategy puzzles where you move one piece and you have to move a dozen others to get the next where you want it. It is not surprising to me that the camera Felipe found last night is sitting precariously on top of the paper shredder. I pick it up by the long lens and ask Danny if he figured out whose it was. He lets out a huge low belch and says No, but whatever fucker left it now has some prime footage of the silverback gorilla in the wild.

What if they come back for it? I ask. You're just gonna give it back to them with that on there? What if it's somebody we like?

It don't show his face, Danny says, just his cock, so what are they gonna do? I think it's pretty fucking funny.

Danny goes home to change into his suit and I try to turn on the camera, thinking I will at least see if I recognize anyone in the noncock photos, but the battery is dead. Later that day I am in the wine cellar updating the eighty-sixed list when the Bishop's handler comes by. The wine cellar is all glass on one side and looks out on the lobby, so I see the handler come in and walk up to the front desk. I wave at him, indicating that I will come out to help him, realizing immediately that the camera is probably the Bishop's. I squat down by a bin, facing away from him, putting the bottles of Silver Oak away very slowly as I imagine saying Sir there are pictures of white cock on your camera or No sir we haven't found a camera but we'll let you know.

If I take out the card before I give it back he'll notice as soon as he gets wherever he's going and it might get back to Danny. If I don't give him the camera and I hang on to it until I can figure out what to do it might get back to Danny. The Bishop calls Danny directly whenever he wants a reservation and Danny is the only person in the restaurant the Bishop will speak to in person, besides Calvin. One thing you can get fired for faster than Danny can unzip his pants is if he hears about something from a guest when you could have told him first. So if I take out the card or I don't give the handler the camera I will have to tell Danny just to cover my ass, and who knows how he will react to my do-gooding. Don't fuck up, I say to myself, don't fuck up. Three weeks ago I took Ana on her first airplane trip ever. Just the two of us, we went to Chicago and had chocolate-chip pancakes across the street from the Art Institute. We built a snow-woman in Grant Park. In the museum, looking at the giant

Impressionist canvas with the people holding umbrellas, my daughter said she thought maybe she would be a painter when she grew up. Or how do you get to work in a museum? she asked. I realize that if I just give the handler the camera the Bishop will never know about the cock photos, because the handler's job is to absorb anything that's pretty fucking funny.

I bet I know what you're here for, I say to the handler as I come out of the wine cellar. The camera?

He says Yes, I don't know how I forgot it, it was a big night for us.

Yes, I say, it's a fine-looking piece of equipment.

———

When that magazine article comes out later and it says the Bishop, just back from a trip to Africa, and the Professor met in this city and found some common ground after years of unfriendliness, and when I show Calvin the part in the article that says this alliance forging began over a long dinner at a steakhouse, we talk about how we know it was that night. You brought that, I tell Calvin, it was your energy, they felt it, they couldn't help but love each other. He doesn't disagree but he hangs his head and his mouth gets tight and he crosses his arms, which is something he does when he's pissed, and he says And look how we treated them with that fucking business, it's shameful. I never brought any shame to this place and they putting it on me like that, it just ain't right.

What's this we? I say. You had nothing to do with it. They don't know we didn't know whose camera it was, but even if they think it *was* hate no way do they think you knew anything about it. It's not on you.

Don't matter, he says, it's all the same. Everything's on everybody.

———

So where I'm going with this is the phone call I took today. They used to come in, the Bishop and the handler, every few weeks, and I didn't see them for months after all that. If I thought about it now and then I hoped I was just missing them on my days off but today the handler called to cancel the Bishop's birthday party in The Private Room, which had been reserved for the purpose ever since the day after his birthday party in The Private Room last year. I didn't ask why they wanted to cancel. I said Thank you sir, even though I didn't know what I was thanking him for. Then I said And please give our best to the Bishop—hope to see you both here again before long. We've missed you.

All right, he said. You the little girl gave me back the camera?

Yes sir, I said.

Thought so. I recognized your voice. You tell Danny he'll never have the Bishop's business again in this life, and he's a sick motherfucker, may God forgive me for cursing a man who has no shame. *No* shame.

Yes sir, I said. I'm sorry, sir. Take care.

I hung up the phone and my neck was hot and it was very quiet in the office.

The fourth and last night in Mexico your father and I drink horchata, sitting on rough-cut logs around a fire. Everyone else has gone to bed after our final worship service, which was held here by the fire. We sang hymns and devotionals and all the stars were out. It is the first time I have seen the Milky Way and I look and look and look.

We stay there as the fire dies, talking. It gets colder and colder so your father goes inside to get his sleeping bag. We wear it around us like a shawl. We keep expecting the youth minister to come looking for us and make us go to bed but he doesn't. I don't think I'll ever be warm again, I say. Your father says Come on, Snowflake. Let's go inside.

Our group has been staying in the church of our host congregation, sleeping on the floor in our sleeping bags. I think he means we will go inside and go to bed, I in the fellowship hall where the girls are and he in the classroom with the boys. But when we enter the church he leads us down the short hallway to the kitchen. Past the kitchen is a door with a picture of a woman kneeling at an altar, praying.

My teeth are chattering as we enter what seems to have been a closet or a pantry before it was converted to a tiny prayer room. On the shelves are books and hymnals and

Bibles. On the floor is a velvet cushion to kneel or sit on, in front of a small table. There are rocks and dried flowers and a small bowl of rice on the table, among other offerings.

We can see only because of the dim filtered starlight coming from the hall; there are no windows. He lights the candles and then closes the door to the hall. He takes the sleeping bag from around my shoulders and quickly zips it back into the shape of a sleeping bag, while stepping out of his boots. Take off your shoes, he whispers. I take them off and put them next to his. The room is only a foot or two longer than the sleeping bag, and not much wider. He pulls back a corner of the sleeping bag and motions for me to get in. He moves the velvet cushion to the top of the sleeping bag, and waits for me to get settled, my head on the makeshift pillow. Then he gets into the sleeping bag too, and zips it up all the way. Hey little Spoon, he says, embracing me. I have never felt so whole, or safe, or known since.

This should warm you up fast, he says. Body heat.

He kisses my neck.

Did you follow me through the gateway, into the blizzard? I whisper.

Yes, Aviendha of the Aiel, he says, playing along. We have both been reading Robert Jordan's *Wheel of Time* series.

I roll over, on top of him. Rand al'Thor, I say into his neck. What's your plan for getting us back?

I don't have one, he says.

———

We wake together when we hear noise in the kitchen on the other side of the wall. He looks at his watch. Six forty-seven, he whispers. Hurry.

We fumble quietly out of the sleeping bag. I put on my shoes and kiss him and put my ear to the door. I don't hear my whole life being written for me inside my body, cell by cell.

———

I burn my neck with a fondue skewer while you watch *The Cosby Show* on my bed. You are watching all two hundred episodes for the second time. You refer to the episodes by sweaters: the one where Vanessa wore the black sweater with the yellow cars. Sondra's flower sweater episode. The skewer is sharp but I don't use the prongs. I turn on the gas burner and hold the metal rod over the blue flicker until the plastic handle begins to feel warm in my fingers and the prongs turn red, devilish. I wait for the laugh track because I know the skin will make a popping crackling sound I don't want you to hear but it would most likely go unnoticed anyway. It would sound like a normal cooking sound. I press the metal rod in hard and let up after a count of three. I put it in the dishwasher, small shreds of skin stuck to it.

It hurts but it feels good. I mean it feels like relief. The pain is real and synchronizes all the pain in the rest of my self that I cannot manage to organize. Draws it up to my neck and tells it what it is: You are pain, this is what you feel like.

When you ask about the greenish bubbled stripe that

appears across the hollow of my clavicular notch I say I think a bug bit me.

You ask to touch it and you are fascinated by how the blister feels full but fragile. You say it's gross but you want to do it again. You are skeptical. You say I should go to the doctor. You say What kind of bug would do that?

———

We can't have pets in my apartment so we put together a jigsaw puzzle of a Saint Bernard on the floor in the hall. You name him Barry, after the legendary Alpine rescue dog. You buy a bag of dog food with your own money and leave bowls of food and water next to him. I hear you apologize to him once when you accidentally step on his tail.

You tell me you have decided you are not going to have children when you grow up. You are going to live in an RV, which you call a house car. You will have two dogs and it will just be the three of you, traveling everywhere with the windows down. You tell me Barry will be too old to go with you. You whisper so his feelings aren't hurt. You ask me if I will take care of him when you leave home and I say I will.

Calvin D. Colson

Cal is a hustler. Maybe he's a type, maybe he's all over Chicago or Atlanta or some other bluesy black place like Memphis, where he's from originally. But his stuff works in Dallas because there's a lot more space around a black man striving here than in those other places. He was king at The Restaurant. First thing he ever said to me was What are you doing crossing the guest like that. Don't ever cross the guest. I was new to The Restaurant and fine dining both, I was serving someone's salad with the wrong hand on the wrong side. I cared about him from that instant. Wanted to please him, got Velcroed to his there's a right way to do this. That was when The Restaurant was my life, when it was all I had, when I'd run away from her. I'd sleep till nine or ten, one big meal before the shift with the paper or a book. Alone, most always alone.

To do a good job at a table you have to care. Whatever show you're doing, wherever else your mind is, you have to put a twist of real on the very end of it. The people are waiting for that and if you don't pull it out they know and they don't like it. Cal did care, or at least he did that show better than anyone. Something in the way he leaned over people, touched their backs even though you're not supposed to do that, it was like they were in his home and he'd say Now what you want to do is put that first bite together with all of it, get you a little tomato, a little that purple onion, and the thing that brings it all together is get you a piece of that basil. Rub it around in that bas*al*mic—mm! Mm. Tell me bout that.

He said a lot of words that way, slightly off. Mama gon kick me to the curve if we touch, he'd say to me as we messed around on my floor in the afternoon. He had a bank job in addition to The Restaurant, something one of his high-rollers made up for him. What he did there was try to look lively in a beautiful suit. Something from Bachrach. He could wear any color and he could put stripes and checks and prints together and it would work because he was puffed up inside it like he was born to win. What I want to know is was that real.

In that restaurant all of us were off. Chipped. Everybody on the way to the curve. Maybe it's the same in a law firm, a nail salon, whatever high or low. Maybe that's just what it is to be alive, you've got that broken sooty piece of something lodged inside you making you veer left.

Calvin was profiled in a local newspaper when they did a piece on great Texas steakhouses. "Mr. Colson provides what he calls an 'old-school' dining experience, part service, part performance, and all professional. Ask for him at The Restaurant or you'll miss out on what fine dining ought to be," the reviewer said. Lissandri gave him a Rolex for that.

If you read up on our level of service you'll find all kinds of uptight lists about not engaging with the guests, don't say your name, don't try to get call parties, don't push anything on the menu over anything else, be formal and anonymous and perfect. Cal broke all those rules and people tipped him outrageous sums for it.

———

One night one of his call parties didn't come through for him, this German-American guy Konstantin who brought in big business clients and left Cal somewhere between fifty and eighty percent on tabs that were never less than five hundred and could push up on four grand depending on how many guys he had with him and what he wanted out of them. On this particular night Konstantin was distracted or drunk when he signed the credit card voucher and tipped Cal $300 on $1,620, a figure that any one of us would have called a good night. Cal called it cheap and called it to Konstantin's face.

See, anybody else would have been fired for that. If a guest says to you Did we take care of you? after paying the bill the only possible answer is an effusive Yes, thank you for asking. Doesn't matter if they didn't. Like it doesn't matter if they've been sitting there for two hours after the dishwasher left for the night, if they say Are we keeping you? the only possible answer is Oh no, sir, the place is yours.

Cal went up to Konstantin in the lobby where he was still working these Japanese guys, trying to get them all in cabs to the strip club, and made it clear he needed to talk to him immediately, and when Konstantin said What's up,

my brother? Cal pulled him aside and opened the check presenter like he found a turd in it and showed it to Konstantin
and said What is this?

Konstantin went all meek and said Oh did I fuck up?
And Cal said I don't know Kon you tell me, but usually I
see something closer to what I'm worth on this line. Is that
what you think I was worth tonight? Something you weren't
happy with? Because it seemed like all your guys had a great
time and it seemed like they was going the way you wanted
em to.

I'm not sure how he got Konstantin to think that the
multimillion-dollar deal he had just closed succeeded in part
because of Cal's excellent service but Konstantin rescribbled
the tip in as $900 and said to Cal Is that more like it? I'm
sorry, my man, I didn't mean anything by it. You know
you're my guy here. And Cal had the audacity to shake his
hand and say stiffly, still trying to be cold, That's what I
thought but I was about to have to let somebody else be your
guy here and Konstantin said I feel you, we straight?

You should have seen Nic Martinez doing his impres-
sion of Konstantin later in the parking lot. A Mexican doing
a German trying to be black. Nic took a puff of Cal's one-
hitter and passed it to Cal and then put his hand on Cal's
biceps and said I feel you Cal my man my brotha my nigg we
straight? You my homey right? You vant a couple more bills?
You vant me to lick your nuts? and then he was laughing
so hard, so crazy, he was leaning over in front of Cal, still
holding on to his arm and coughing from the big hit he was
trying to hold in and say at the same time Teach me how to
get my own German, massa! Teach me!

Cal was holding up straight, letting a smile stay in his cheeks but looking at his pipe all serious, knocking the cache out, reloading. I know he knew his muscle was popping out strong with Nic hanging on him like that and he took pride in that and pride in his balls-out way with "his people," as he called his call parties. Ain't nothing to teach, he said to Nic, just got to be you and bring it.

He looked bronze with the streetlight shining on him, reflecting off his white undershirt. He looked the same color as Nic but he was really a goldish cinnamon. He said he was ochre, terra-cotta, and sepia, colors a former girlfriend, a painter, gave him. He liked that. He was always painting himself for me.

I mean did he really feel that way about himself though— the way he made it look in the bank suit, the way he made it look with Nic hanging on him. Where was the nugget you couldn't massage or change or put a pinstripe on and was it that confident. Was that kernel whole and well or was it sad, smacked out, lost. I don't know but I think a showman is all show. There's no secret—or there is, and that's it. Like when I asked Danny if that scotch rep Alyssa's tits were real and he said Yeah they're real—real fake.

Cal would have a little taste, as he called it, near the end of the shift when nobody was looking, a taste of Grand Marnier neat. Danny didn't care as long as the guests didn't see and Danny was usually drinking with him anyway. Cal's taste would become two or three tastes and then he would get so frisky, he would start touching all the women—servers, guests, the pastry chef—like you trail your hand through cattails out on a skiff. Pleased, enjoying the weather, nature.

One night after a few tastes he sat down with Doc Melton's woman—Doc wasn't there, and Doc was one of his big men, the ones who kept him on a sick and regular payroll of inflated gratuities at The Restaurant and threw in extras like Mavs tickets. Cal sat down with Cassandra Melton and he told me all about how he felt her up under the table, his fingers on her pussy lips, how fluffed and slick they were and how she sat into it delicately. He did this and after she and her girlfriends left, after he kissed her on each cheek, he came over to me and Danny where we were doing tequila shots at the corner of the bar. He was flying. Oh my Gawd, he said touching his fingers to his lips, that pussy. I can't believe I haven't been getting none of that. Why don't you Cal, I asked, why don't you just take it, always complaining about how long it's been since somebody took care of you at home. Fuck knows it's on offer for you everywhere you go.

No, he said. Can't do that. I'll touch me some titties and some pussy but I won't do *that*. Cal, that is such bullshit, I said, and he said You just say that because you want me to cross over. I do want you to cross over, I said, but it's still bull.

———

That was the summer Cal would come over to my apartment after he got off from the bank, before we had to be in at The Restaurant. Those were warm afternoons, my apartment toasting the Texas sun through big old perfect windows. I moved into that place when I saw the money I was making at The Restaurant. I bought that car too. You can make good money—high fives if you really push, low sixes if you're Cal—but you never lose the feeling that it's fragile, your connection to the money. That place I lived in after I first got that connection, it was small and expensive but it was clean and bright and everything was nice. The carpet was thick and new and Cal and I would scuffle on it every afternoon. His kisses. His face—so soft—Your face! I'd say—I take care of myself, Mami, it's what you got to do he'd murmur—his lips hot, fresh.

That much he allowed. But even if he was stripped down, his suit draped carefully across the back of the loveseat, his white V-neck undershirt tucked into his white boxer briefs, he wouldn't allow me to touch him. I reached and he said No, don't do that. We can't. Mama gon kick me to the curve, I might as well move in.

Okay, I said, move in. I'm ready.

You not ready. You don't know. Why you always want more.

You want it too.

I do. No doubt. But you think we ought to touch outside of our want?

He was forty-four and I was twenty-two but he was in better shape. His waist as trim as mine, his pecs tortoise-shells, his quads modeling those boxer briefs. Before The Restaurant he used to train the Highland Park moms at Gold's. He still got up at four every day to do his reps—pushups, crunches, curls—before his daughter woke, then he'd make breakfast and take her to school. That was his time with her. Home late, never to bed before two or three in the morning, the office afternoon would fall on him like a tree. Him in that bank chair, sleeping upright in that suit.

So his excuse for coming over was he needed a nap. Only once did we actually nap—or he did, sleeping clean and gentle in his whites. I lay behind him, my hand on his thigh, breathing in the warm buttery smell of his neck, afraid to move, afraid to sleep and miss his sleeping in my arms, as if he were a comet, an eclipse, a papal visit. Not just a man pausing on me, a bead in his rosary.

But usually we rolled around on the floor, I listened to him talk, I begged for it, then I'd give up and go take a shower and he'd watch me start to finish, hand me the towel. Once he said You got a body too. Baby Rie-rie, lil M, look at those big nipples she got. Ugh. I could work with those big gumdrops and that bush. Real woman got a bushy bush like that, don't know what all this mess with some naked pussy lips is for.

Don't talk about it if you don't want it, I said. You're not for real. I'm for real. I'm ready.

You sure not ready for work, he said, looking at his watch, changing the subject. Looking at his fingernails. He got them buffed every Saturday, they were always shiny. His shoes too. He'd drop off one pair and pick up another. He had some military standards. He believed in the power of systems and order to manifest success. He believed in every clichéd thing about the power of belief. He believed in believing in belief. I tell my baby she not allowed to use the word can't, he said. And he said I don't get sick cause I just refuse to. You tell yourself Oh I'm sick—he said this in a whiny puny voice, screwing up his face—you sure enough will be.

That swaggering, who knew it wasn't his belief in himself that made it all go. That it did work if you worked it. I was never that certain about anything. That's your problem, he said, you doubt yourself. You got to want it. I do want it, I said. Nah you don't. Not if you don't know you want it. What's that big dark thing behind you? he said, and I said I don't know, what, showing him I was impatient with whatever lesson was coming. That's the shadow of a doubt and you best deal with it right here right now.

What I wanted was some jack. Make that jack, baby, make that jack. Another of his mantras. I got to get out there and make that jack, he said in the back station at The Restaurant, taking a long draw of his protein-ginseng-vitamin smoothie before heading out into the dining room with purpose. I wanted to know how to do what he did. Conjury. Turning dinner into livelihood, wealth, stability. My girl lived in a one-bedroom apartment with her dad, she slept on a futon in the living room. Cal's daughter lived in a giant suburban house with both her parents and took ballet. It's not that I even wanted a giant suburban house for her. I just wanted her to have something from me, anything better than absence.

Cal's daughter Elena, he got her in with this modeling agency. That was him—that belief in the most pressing uniqueness of his own life. No question. My daughter was beautiful too, at three she had flossy red hair down to her waist and strangers would use adult beauty words to describe her, like gorgeous. But I was always thinking something like *Nothing is really all that special.*

Cal was always thinking the opposite. And his daughter was what modeling agencies look for these days, a mixed-race child with fluffy hair and skin that one caramel Polynesian shade. She was tall, five feet when she was eight, with long delicate bones. Like Cal's having her in ballet and modeling from the time she was small made her that way or something. Like he willed it. He said Man, Maxine will not have that talk with her and I keep getting on to her, telling her it should be a young lady's mother has that talk. She's dangerous, she looks too old, boys gonna be after her in a minute and she so young inside still. I told Max she don't talk to her by her next birthday I'm gonna do it my own self, he said.

Max was Mexican, from Laredo. Cal said After my first marriage I knew the next one would be outside my race, but he never explained that or how he knew. His first wife Tamara was a black woman; they had a baby that was stillborn and took the marriage with it. Angeline, tattooed on his heart, scroll, script.

——

I was always moving the furniture around in that apartment. Couldn't get situated. There was a beige velvet loveseat from 1974, which my parents bought the year they married and kept for thirty more. With that kind of example you'd think I wouldn't have turned out so transient, you'd think I'd have been more like Cal, rooted, a straight line from point of origin up. There wasn't anything wrong with the couch when I got it and it seemed like I should have had that kind of unblemished momentum too, considering who I came from. I put it in the dining room until I made enough jack to get a tiny bistro table at a restaurant supply store. By then

I felt like I had been living in restaurants forever and would never escape so I don't know why I wanted to feel restaurant at home too. I had thick ceramic café mugs and those standard restaurant highballs and pint glasses. I had those bar towels, white with the single red stripe. The aesthetics of high volume are usually durable and plain I suppose. Plain itself is durable and that appealed to me, so I didn't deploy the theater that Calvin unfurled on his tables. I didn't even give them my card at the end of the meal. I never said Ask for me next time. Cal was pushy about that, made them feel like they'd be dumb if they didn't.

First the loveseat was in the dining room, that's where Cal told me about Angeline and I told him about how I'd married my daughter's dad when I was seventeen because my own dad hit me for the first and only time. Whacked the side of my head and said we needed to plan a wedding before I started showing. I went along but when she was three I left. Her dad's a good guy and I love her like nothing. Neither of those changed the fact that I'd felt crazy since she was born, like I wasn't meant for it. I just woke up one day and said I can't do this. This isn't real. I'm in the wrong life. It was that abrupt, overnight, like a snake molting out of a skin. Leaving it behind, slithering away cold-blooded.

When I got the table for the dining room I moved the loveseat into the living room, canted to face the corner. But after Ryan Doak broke my bed frame trying to fuck Iraq out of himself I moved the mattress into the living room as if the place were a loft and put the loveseat in my bedroom. The bed that broke I got from my parents too, and it was an antique mahogany four-poster, even older than the loveseat. I'd been staring at the geometric inlay on that headboard since I could remember.

It was when the mattress was there in the living room, its last stop, that I had to talk to Max on the phone. Cal called me and said Listen I need you to talk to Max. He said it in such a way that I knew she was right there and it was over. I talked to her on my back on the mattress and I'm afraid I sounded like a junkie. Laconic. In a call center you're not supposed to lean back in your chair if you're trying to sell something, you're supposed to sit up straight and pretend the person can see you. It affects how you talk. I should have sat up. I think I said what I was supposed to say to her but my rebellion was lying down so she'd hear some other thing in my voice, hear some tip tap of the truth.

I was supposed to say and did say Nothing is going on with me and your husband even though he had a $600 cell phone bill last month, and it was all calls to me. The thing I shake my head over now is how for probably $589 worth of that $600 I couldn't understand what he was saying, I was just listening. He would talk, he would fall into a chant, and something about his mellow voice and his way of speaking and the connection combined to make him unintelligible. I just said Uh huh and Oh yeah? or whatever was called for by the tone. But I didn't think it would make sense if I said to Max I'm sorry the phone bill was so high but trust me I don't even know what he said to me. And I couldn't say Yes—your instincts—what you cannot think on has most definitely occurred, I have been heavily petted by Calvin D. Colson every day for three months, and your husband was in his underwear, but he wouldn't let me touch his cock. I didn't figure that last would give any comfort. And I knew Cal would kill me if I said anything real.

That was the contradiction, that's what I'm trying to get at. He took it for granted that you would do some things that just weren't straight, and he took it for granted that that was justified. I guess that's corruption. Riding those actions like a boss. One afternoon before the afternoons ended he brought me a twenty-bag. He knew I'd gone back to coke even if I wasn't giving it up to everybody anymore. He couldn't believe I hadn't gotten pregnant or caught something during all that. Young lady, you got some kind of angel looking out for you, he said. But the main reason I was keeping it to myself was so I could have a chance with him, because I knew he would never go there with me if he caught the scent of anybody else. I let him think I was learning how to be a woman, as he put it, instead of just trying to get what I wanted from him.

He said the coke was from the Baron. The Baron was this Turkish guy who pretended to be Italian and dropped by The Restaurant once or twice a year. He'd show up like we'd been waiting for him and no one else through all that intervening time, each of us frozen in uniform, in place, until his presence disseminated some magic dust to make us come alive again so we could fulfill our destinies of serving him. The magic dust was some green and some white and all handshook. I'm sure Cal got the don's share of both and he told me he kept the bags to pass on to his people, just like he kept cigarettes and disposable cameras in his locker for when they ran out of smokes or got engaged. Once I even saw him fix a lady's dress with a safety pin he had in his pocket.

I never knew anybody who kept coke though, which is the main fissure in my Cal wall. It's a terrible habit but I tend to believe what people tell me, so when he told me the story of how years ago he quit using crack and coke I believed it. Then he gives me that twenty-bag and tells me he got it from the Baron and he's been keeping it under the floor mat in his BMW. I looked at him and thought You don't make your daughter breakfast and you're fucking Cassandra Melton and you didn't quit partying and you're not going to make it. I looked at him and looked away and I cut it into lines on top of a drawing my daughter made, the two of us portrayed as lean and grinning neighbors in one of those stick-figure sketches that seemed more a demand for normalcy than a depiction of the actual. This is the kind of obstinate I was. I thought it was bad form to lay it out on her little picture like that, like it seemed too obvious a send-up of my failings, like I ought to keep her effort sacred if only out of superstition. But that's what I wanted to face down—mine was an inversion of Cal's *just got to be you and bring it.* I wouldn't let myself look away from what I was doing and to punish myself for seeing it I wouldn't let myself fix it. Sometimes I would get home from work and I would get stuck in the car, just sitting there in the carport looking out over the steering wheel. An hour could pass as I watched the security light come on and go off as the bars let out, flushing cars up Greenville Avenue.

I did one line and Cal told me not to touch the rest till I saw what happened, said it was real shit and all I'd ever had was baby laxative because he knew I got it from the Mexicans at work. I don't know why I listened to him, that wasn't my practice usually, but within about thirty seconds my brain had melted. Why did you just do that to me, I said, sounding to myself like the gigantic demented rabbit in *Donnie Darko*. Why did you do that why did you do that why did you do that, I said. My face was falling apart. My face is falling off, I said to him, my face is falling falling you fucking cunt. You did that to me on purpose.

I didn't do shit, he said, you the one did the line just now when you know you got to be at work! How you gonna work now? How you gonna drive?

What is all your talk about coming through for yourself, showing up, flying right if you're gonna sabotage me like this?

You sabotaged yourself! Coulda waited till after work or done anything in the world with that. I asked you if you wanted it and you coulda said no! Don't blame this on me. You do gotta show up and fly right in your own life or you gonna lose everything.

How can somebody who rubs his fingers all over every woman he passes and wonders why his wife won't put out talk to me about fly right?

This contorted exchange continued until Cal said Look I got to go, I got to get ready myself. You better get it together. You shouldn't be doin that stuff you don't know how to snap out.

Get the fuck out with your goddamned *I can be sober if I want cause I'm such a badass* voodoo! I said.

He left. I went into the kitchen and turned on a burner.

I had slipped into such synesthesia that the clicking of the pilot made me have an orgasm. Propped on the back of the stove was a piece of a broken mirror, a mirror I broke when I moved into that apartment. In the piece of mirror, which was shaped like Tennessee, my irises were gone. All-pupil looks vacant and deadly. And my movements had contrails as I looked away from the mirror and opened a drawer to find a steak knife. I heated the blade over the flame and then raised my cocktail dress—this was back when I still worked mostly in the bar at The Restaurant—and pulled down my panty hose to get to my abdomen. I burned Cal's initials into the skin to the right of my navel, each about one inch square and made of straight lines, like letters carved into a tree. I felt and did not feel the pain. Skin melts like wax. I cut a big hole in the waist of the pantyhose so I could pull them back up and they wouldn't stick to the wound.

I don't know how I drove to work, all I remember is I had to sit down with Danny in the office and explain to him why I couldn't close my mouth or stop crying. I said something about my daughter. What I said was true, in the sense that it's true that that kind of coke will napalm your emotional synapses and whatever you care about most will suddenly be getting a sky's worth of air.

————

Why isn't she with you? Cal had asked me on one of the first afternoons when we were getting to know each other. I don't know what to give her, I said. Bullshit, he said, you give her love, you give her time, you give her attention. Is that what you give Elena, I asked. Much as I can, he said. I want to do it right, I said, not much as I can right, just right.

You got to do it some kinda way to start, he said.

———

Danny let me go home the day I did the Baron's line—it wasn't the first time he granted me some clemency when he knew what was up, I don't know why. He'd fire anybody for nothing. I guess he could keep people around on the same capriciousness but he said to me once that I was golden there. I was worried because we fucked up Doc Melton's sea bass and his mom's pork loin all in one night. Neither was my fault but that never mattered. Honey, you're golden here, Danny said to me, don't worry about it. We could have served that old bitch cat meat and she probably would have loved it.

Cal wouldn't look at me as I passed him on my way out the day I went home blitzed. He pulled this junk where we'd be cuddling and playing and necking and laughing at three p.m. upstairs on the corner of Morningside and Greenville and at six p.m. under the domed ceiling of The Restaurant suddenly he was tired, he was busy, he was clipped and distant. I think it was even worse that day because he didn't want to acknowledge any connection to the wreck of me. He did not shift his gaze to look at me as I left; he was looking up at the specials board dutifully copying down the features and counts. Made that look like the most important thing a body could be doing. I saw his fingers roll the pen slightly and that was what said *I see you but I want you to know I'm not looking at you.* I imagined slapping his waiter book from his hand on my way out. It would fly down on the floor, he'd suck his teeth and bend over like a man who'd been working in restaurants for three decades, because he had. Mindful of the back, a slow careful squat of the legs. He'd give me a disgusted look over his shoulder, a shake of his head, eternal dismissal. I would never be loved again. At least until tomorrow afternoon. I knew his routine by then, but I didn't whack the book because I thought I might fall down.

On the nights that Cal and I were both at The Restaurant it was agreed between us that we couldn't leave without tracking down the other to say good night. I did it once, just finished my shit and left, and he called me the next day. Said What you think you doin walking out without saying good night to me? I couldn't find you, I said. Lame, he said, that's a weak-ass excuse. You got any more weak-ass excuses for me today? No sir, I said. Good, he said, you can walk out whenever you want I'm not there, and I don't care who else you don't say good night to but don't be like that with me. Okay, I said. All right missy, I got to run back into this bank, will I see you tonight? Yes, I said, love you. Love you back, he said. I always knew I was good with him if he said I love you back, not I love you too. If he ever said I love you too it meant I'm unhappy with you, I don't feel it, it meant I'm just talking to you, meant My mouth is making some meaningless sounds. I love you too meant nothing so much it almost meant I don't love you.

I didn't even try to speak to him as I walked out that day. If I'd said Bye Cal, love you see you later he probably

wouldn't have even said I love you too. He would have said
Mm-hmm. Or just Mm.

Fuck him. Fuck him back and fuck him too and fuck
him, I thought. I called my friend Clark, a beautiful speci-
men of a man who used to be a licensed chemical depen-
dency counselor before he left that behind to deal the most
divine hydro. I wanted to come down as fast as possible and I
wanted someone to take care of me. I wanted to hide my self
somewhere where I couldn't get to it. I wanted someone to
take it from me, let me think it was safe. How dumb. He got
me stoned but it didn't put my face back together at all. I still
felt razed. I almost latched on to a Shirley Horn album but
missed. I sat in the bottom of the shower forever, water running over me and taking nothing with it. He left for a previously arranged dinner with a friend and I felt abandoned.
My teeth sang.

I did not sleep. I stared at the ceiling in Clark's place, to
which was affixed a tapestry with a giant embroidered *om*
character. Clark came home from the dinner around three
a.m. and I begged him to get me some narcotics so I could
have eyelids again. He said he didn't know where to get any.
I was lying naked on the bed, covered partly by a towel and
partly by the clothes I was clutching but hadn't been able to
put on. He asked me what happened here, where CDC was
illegible for blisters I knew would deflate and turn to pus the
next day, from having branded myself with lesser, simpler
marks in other places. I said Calvin D. Colson, Calvin D.
Colson, ochre, terra-cotta, golden Colson.

He said Shh, he said I can't get you any narcotics but I
would like to make love to you. I don't know if that would

have any palliative effect but I would really like to. I said All right, but I'm having trouble controlling my face. He said that was fine, he laughed, he kissed me tenderly, his long hair fell over me. Clark was slender, he had a white man's no-ass, not those two baby heads in a sack like Cal. He had a large thick straight penis and any time we did it he was in it all the way, studying it like a lepidopterist, admiring every intricate pattern up close with gravity and joy. His intensity pulled me down and down and down until I came and slept.

———

Cal would bring Max and Elena into the restaurant so they could all have dinner there once in a while, on special occasions like when he finished his cleansing. The cleansing was an annual thing, Christmas through April or something like that, and he cut out meat, cheese, alcohol, sugar, and weed. I teased him after he first delivered that list—And I know you're still not getting any so what you got left for yourself my friend?—and he said Yes ma'am you have a point there but it's about purification. And let me tell you how good that long bone cowboy tastes come April.

When he brought in the family I steered clear. Everybody else would go by the table to coo over his baby and be kind to the wife but I knew I couldn't. Avoiding her had never been hard until one Valentine's Day long after Cal's summer with me. By then they'd made him a manager and I was see-ing the hateful man, unhappily. I came into work later than everyone that day because Danny had asked me to pick up his suits and some razor blades on my way in, so I missed the introduction of Max in the shift meeting. Valentine's

Day meant twice as many covers, the dining room converted into a sea of deuces, people jammed into three square feet of space to wait forever for their steak and stare into each other's eyes drumming up some juice for whatever came next. So they brought in some extra hands to run food and polish glasses, but I didn't know Cal had conscripted Max until sometime around what would be the sixth or seventh second of a bull ride, time to hold on tight to that shift or give up, fall off. I had a station far from provisions so every time someone dropped a napkin or a spoon or needed more sauce, more ice, more butter, I was hauling myself to go get, go get, go get, but I was hanging on, that's why Cal put me back there, because it would have been a disaster with some of the baby servers or fuckups in that station.

I had my hands full of some dishes I had cleared, and a bottle of wine and a check presenter tucked under one arm, when this lady at one of my tables asked if I could please get her some creamy horseradish. Certainly, I said, right away, attempting to hold the stack of dishes away from her but unable to do anything more than gesture at that without putting the gristly remains of a ribeye in the face of the large man at my other elbow. As I twisted, I saw a woman in a sort-of uniform behind me—the same white shirt and apron as me, without the vest and tie—so I assumed she was one of the add-ons they'd brought in for the night and before I took a good look at her face I asked her if she could take the plates please. Then I was looking into her pretty brown eyes and I knew from Cal's wallet exactly who she was, and she was looking at me thinking she knew who I must be just from process of elimination—there weren't that many girls who worked at The Restaurant—and from the kind of questions a wife asks a man about the other, in those moments when she's thinking she can deal with it: What does she look like? Is she white? Trying to find out if she's hot or young or has big tits. And the husband will answer with thin lips. He's fucked so he'll say things like Why you got to know all this, what's it matter, instead of answering, and she'll say things like I just want to know why I'm not enough for you.

Then he'll sigh and say She has short hair and she could never give me what you do. There. Is that all?

In the dark dining room I guess she couldn't see my face cook up to a warm red medium-rare, something a white girl can't hide. Not that I regretted any second I'd spent with Cal. What I regretted was having just asked her to do me a favor when I hadn't done her any, but there was no time to think about that if I was going to stay on the bull, no time to do anything but try to get that woman her creamy horseradish while she still had a bite or two of filet mignon to enjoy with it.

Men will toy with you, I don't care how much they talk about a woman being a tease. Married men will. Single men rarely hesitate past a certain point. But married men will toy, treat you like you're plastic, like whatever grip you have on whatever kind of heart you have is your business, like maybe you don't even have anything that could be offended. I think that's the same scared-boy coin though—single man on the one side taking what he can, married man on the other afraid to mess up what he took.

So I'd let Cal do what he would, I'd left him alone. What I wanted was his want and that's not something you can force. But after I dropped off that sauce I went to put back the bottle of wine and he was at the POS there, sweating. Past four hundred covers and he'd be moving so fast and holding so much in his brain and taking so much shit from guests that his ochre forehead would start to run. A gentleman, he patted, with a folded linen that matched his suit. Think you're hot! I said to him, Guess who I just met in the dining room? Fucking give a sister a tip, you know?

I wasn't slowing down to hear his piece, just gliding behind him to put that pinot in its bin and get back out to my corner, but I'd picked the wrong place in his night to be tough, I was probably the latest of nineteen people to yell at him and I wasn't in line to spend a couple bills on dinner so I didn't merit any deference. I was just supposed to do my job and not cause trouble. Hey! he said, like he'd say to a dog that was in his bushes or a hood trying to steal his kid's bike, that Hey! full of strange to cut me, You better get back here and pump that, I don't care how busy you are!

That was how he knew to get to me, ignore what I said and go for my work, imply that I was lazy, that I didn't have standards as good as his. I went back. I took the bottle out of the bin and put the white plastic pump on the rubber stopper and pumped the air out of it and said to him Cal, I swear to God you did not pump your wine on a night like this when you were a server and if you tell me you did I'm going back out there to find her and I'm going to tell her I sucked every drop out of you every day and I'm going to tell her I'm still doing it and you're a fucking liar and I'll explain to her that that's because you fuck me and you lie to her.

He was quiet. Then What in hell is up with you? he

said, aware that the situation suddenly required more than a power play. Nic walked up needing something from Cal then but Cal didn't turn to him, and looked at me long as I walked away. Come talk to me later he said, putting some suspicion in there for a buffer but some respect too, to tempt me.

Once I did get one lick. I surprised him and I got there before he could block me. I got one lick on the underside of his big vitiligoed head and he pushed me away instantly, strongly, said The fuck you doing! just the way he'd said Hey! trying to squash me so I'd never do that again. Then seeing the look on my face, both the want and the apology, he'd said Mami, don't do that. I'll spill. As if to say If I promise I want you more than anything will you accept nothing.

———

You get tired of being a fixture in a restaurant every night, even if like me you somehow love the job. Something about the word waitress too that always bothered me, made my lower belly quiver in that bad way, like when you walk through a nursing home. I quit The Restaurant the day I waited on Carter Wells and he asked me what I would do if I could do anything right this second, if money were no object. I said as I poured the taste, a swirl of the $800 Lafite Rothschild he'd ordered even though he was alone, Sir money is an object and could never be else but if money were no *obstacle* I'd live in a place where my little girl could go to a good school. Or maybe I wouldn't even make her go to school, maybe we'd just see the world together from your side of the table.

With this I raised the glass with its swirl as if to toast the imaginary gift of an imaginary life and I put my whole small face inside the bowl and inhaled and then I drank that wine and said You enjoy your evening and I walked out of The Restaurant, holding the glass in my hand.

No. I would never do that.

But believe me that move is not original in the business. I knew a guy who did that in Morton's one night, they have a spiel with a cart and all these props, and there's a part where you have to hold up a potato and talk about what they can do with it. He held up the potato and—I can't do this, he said, and put the potato down and left. He told me After you do it it feels like the stupidest thing because most likely you just end up in some other restaurant holding some other potato but way behind on your rent.

I did think about it though. Especially late at night when I was so hungry. Around ten thirty or eleven when I'd been at work for hours and hadn't eaten since lunch, and the place was still brutally busy so I knew I wouldn't eat until one or two in the morning. Then I would be running some steaming potatoes au gratin to some table and I'd think If I ever walk out this is how: Step up to the table with that bowl and instead of serving them stand there spooning the hot buttery crumbly cheesy potatoes into my mouth. We all became scavengers late at night. The law may require a lunch break but how are you going to take a lunch break at the height of service? At midnight I'd see a half-eaten dish of potatoes on the edge of a deuce in the bar and I'd catch their server's eye. She knew what I wanted because she wanted it too. She'd start bussing the table in that ungodly sexy way she had, leaning over with her luscious tits in their nose, asking if they wanted dessert and laughing when they said As long as it's you, like she didn't hear that every night. I'd meet her in the back and we'd hide behind the glass polisher, scarfing. If Danny came into the back the glass polisher would yell Hola jefe and one of us would turn nonchalantly to the sink to wash our hands while the other began carefully creating an upside-down bouquet of stemware to carry back into the bar. We'd leave the last bites of the potatoes for the glass polisher.

People had been punished and fired for eating in the restaurant, surrounded by food. So most nights I didn't risk it. I just finished my work and went home and went to bed, too tired to eat but not too hungry to sleep.

When I walk across the stage as valedictorian six weeks after the mission trip I still don't know. I didn't track my cycle very closely and the end of high school is a busy time. My parents invite everyone from church to a backyard barbecue to celebrate my acceptance to Yale. I have visited New Haven and met some of my professors. I sat in Sterling Memorial Library and read from Shusaku Endo's *Silence* and thought about your dad but I was about to do something no one I knew had done, and there was no way for him to come with me.

I also thought that what we had done was wrong.

———

The elders accept the youth minister's resignation. In his letter to the congregation he says that he deeply regrets having failed to safeguard the children in his care, referring to me I suppose.

The elders meet with me privately, in the library. Nine of them and a seventeen-year-old girl. Well, you're the last person we'd have expected this to happen to, one says. Now, I don't know what the circumstances were, says another, and you don't have to tell us. But we all know how young men are. Ultimately it's you girls who have to decide, who have to make choices to stay in the straight and narrow when it comes to purity.

I am so ashamed, so mortified, that I leave myself there at the table. I make myself four inches tall and I wing over to a bookshelf in a far corner. I alight on the highest shelf and look down at the girl in the red tank top. Her hair obscures her face and she stares at the table, trembling. I don't know her, and I don't know these men in dark suits, and there is nothing I can do to help her. She is too small, and there are nine of them. I tiptoe behind a book and lie down. I turn away from the room and fall asleep.

———

I wake up in my room at home. I feel the thick woozy tiredness that is new to me because I have never been pregnant before.

———

I didn't take personally anything The Restaurant ever had in store for me. I just did the next thing as well as I could and then the next. The fifth or sixth sous-chef I worked with was griping at Florida John one night over some mess that had gone down earlier in the evening, when I walked up to restock some plates. Why can't you be like this one? said the sous-chef, putting his hand on my shoulder. Don't matter what happens out there, she's ice. What's your secret? he asked. Enlighten this motherfucker.

Accept that shit is all fucked up and roll with it, I said.

Don't bitch. Just adapt. Nothing is going to go right and everything is going to be hard.

Jesus, Confucius, said the sous-chef.

———

You crawl in bed with me in the middle of the night. You put your little arm on my chest and say you are afraid I'm going to die while I'm sleeping. I say You're not afraid I'm going to die while I'm awake?

When you're awake I can keep an eye on you, you say.

No, that doesn't make sense, I say. You mean that when *you're* awake you can keep an eye on me.

No, when I'm sleeping and you're awake I dream about what you're doing, you explain. But when you're sleeping I never know.

The Private Room

Tonight they've put me on thirty men in The Private Room. The men are all white, fat, and over fifty. Sometimes parties like this will show up all at once on a hotel bus or in a drove of limos, if they're in town for a convention and everything is organized. But these guys trickle in, and by the time the last few arrive some of them have already been drinking for two hours. DeMarcus, my partner on the party, got everything started—introduced us, went over the set menu, helped them pick out their wine.

I wonder if it's a good thing that DeMarcus will be the face and I'll be backwaiting. You get to know the look of new money and the look of old; you can call on sight, with near-perfect accuracy, whether a person is a martini, a red wine, a Stella, a *Just water no ice extra lemon and a straw did I say no ice?;* you know that certain European accents doom your take. You have an entire catalogue of these things in your head but still there will come that table, they're wearing jeans and when you ask them what they want to drink they say two Diet Cokes and an iced tea and you think you know what you're in for—an appetizer as an entrée, split three ways, ten percent on a tab that's missing a couple digits. They're making out at the table, he looks twice her age, you can't figure out why the other one is with them. *Low-class,* you think, *guess it's not my night.* Then you walk up with the second basket of bread they asked for and they say to bring out a bottle of Dom Rosé. After that they drink the 2000 Harlan Estate and order the big lobster tail. You start moving like you've got somewhere to be and when the bartender tries to play around with you instead of handing over the decanter you snap at him because if they come through you stand to make $500 off a three-top.

Same thing with these types in The Private Room, the unpredictability. Sometimes they want a girl with their steak—a rival establishment across town employs only women—and sometimes they don't think a girl can do the job, or they seem embarrassed for you.

I won't be talking much from here on out, and with the look of them I'm glad of that even if it might have worked out better for us with me up front. I fill their wineglasses and pick up the cocktail napkins they've brought with them from the bar. Are you ready for another, sir? I say. One of them has already downed three Jack 'n' waters and the hors d'oeuvres haven't even arrived. His nose is red and his eyes are pushed deep into a big waxy face. I ring up another for him and when I head into the well to pick it up DeMarcus is there, loading some other cocktails onto a tray. I point at the Jack and ask him if he'll take it with him so I can prep some mise en place. Who's it goin to? he asks. You know, I say, Lushie. Ah, he says, big fella? They're all big, I say. Well, they're all lushies too, he says.

Back in the room Lushie is standing, whiskey in hand, inviting everyone else to sit. He starts talking about their colleague who passed recently, due to an aortal aneurism. You can tell the others think this is a downer. They just got going on their buzz and they have to tell it to hold on a minute because it's making them want to laugh when they should be serious, so they start playing with their forks and staring at the tablecloth and they start drinking even harder. You look down the table and the arms and glasses are going up and down quietly but nonstop like derricks. Lushie is using long medical terms with the somber educated air of a preacher bringing the word. *The word is—what? I think. Heartsick? Moderation? Death? Quit it all right now?*

Finally he drains his glass and sits all in one motion and the chatter folds back in around us and I can tell some of them feel like they barely made it out. Now they're talking *merger*, *due diligence*, *cash flow*, *liquidity*, *execute*, and the deadly *amortization*. I have my language too, so though I think about asking Lushie if he wants me to mainline it for him I put it the nice way and say with a prompting lilt in my voice, Would you like me to keep those coming for you sir? and I start making them double-talls to slow him down, something Cal taught me. *He wants to drink let him drink, and make him pay for it too—he feels that second or third double hit his ass and he don't slow down, more power to him. But you don't got to be running around for him like his goddamn lil bitch.*

We take the order, DeMarcus on one side of the table and I on the other. We have an unspoken rivalry about who can get from position one to position fifteen the fastest. The pros get the order taking down to a call-and-response that reads each guest's mind and draws out his selections for three courses with all pertinent temperatures and modifications in forty-five seconds or less, without letting him feel the slightest bit rushed. You expand your intake words, like Certainly and Absolutely and That won't be a problem, sir, you let them hang rich and pillowy in a smile and the guest thinks only of how accommodating and efficient you are, he doesn't hear the ticking of the giant railroad clock in your head that is Chef, waiting on the line for this order because a big party will affect the cook times for everything in the house. I'm one position behind DeMarcus, since one of my guys takes forever to acknowledge me, even though I'm standing there next to him saying Sir? Sir? Have you had a chance to decide? At some point you have to give up and wait for the friends he's talking to to advocate for you, give him a sign with their eyes that he's being rude to you. I hear DeMarcus talking to his seat eight about what vegetables he wants on the table for the party. This guy calls him Mark—DeMarcus is sensitive about his name, at least in the restaurant, and I don't blame him. He'll truncate it like that if he feels he needs to, though I think his name sounds regal and hip in the parking lot late at night when his brother swings by to get him and they ask me to climb in for a puff. On my side, on Lushie's right, there's one black guy. Guess he's their EEOC compliance. He's the only one of the lot who doesn't order a steak—he asks for the salmon, well-done, and wants to make sure some greens will be on the table. Then I bend over by Lushie's ear to get his order, and he does that thing fat people do where they sit facing forward but they tilt their head back and up toward you like a flower looking for the sun. He says he'll have the ribeye. Maybe he's thinking the same thing I am about that because when I ask him what he'll have for dessert he pauses piously and says, I don't believe I'll have dessert tonight. I'll pass. You'll pass, okay, I say seriously while making notes like a doctor.

I leave the room to ring up my half of the table and while I'm at the POS my friend Asami comes up behind me. I've got some fucking Martians tonight, she says. I know, I say, they're everywhere, and I debrief her about The Private Room. She's telling me these stupid Botoxies at her table are doing the Sandra Oh thing to her again. It always goes down the same way. The ladies see her and she's taking their cocktail order and one of them says to another, Oh you know who she reminds me of? and then turns to Asami and says You know who you look just like? and Asami usually gives them this big gorgeous grin and says *I bet I know exactly what you're thinking,* or *No! I have no idea, who's that?* but she's telling me that tonight instead she kind of lost it and she said to them, I don't look anything *like* Sandra Oh, she's Korean! But I don't look anything like her anyway!

Back in the room I'm clearing the hors d'oeuvres and getting everybody cleaned up and ready for the salad course when the boss stands and starts telling jokes. The boss is the one DeMarcus spoke to at the beginning about the wine, the one who ordered the vegetables—he'll be paying the tab and apparently the reason for this fête is some deal he signed with Lushie. I lent them my pen earlier when they set the contract down in front of him and he started patting his pockets. So two doctors are banging this nurse, he says. She gets pregnant but she doesn't tell them till she's seven months gone, so they send her to Florida to have the baby. They're gonna figure out how to raise it and do right, and of course she'll come back to work at a much higher salary than before because they both have wives and kids. So she delivers and one doc calls the other and says he has bad news. What's that, says the other doc. Well, she had twins, says the first doc, and mine died!

Grinning, he lets the laughter die down and then he goes, Okay, how bout this one. So one doctor says to the other, Are you fucking the nurse? The other doctor says No, why? And the first doctor says, Good! You fire her!

Now he rides the laughter, shouting How do you know your wife is dead? Sex is the same but the dishes start to pile up!

I catch DeMarcus's eye across the table and I can see the laugh he's stifling pulling at the corners of his mouth. He gives me a look like *What are you gonna do? It's funny,* and I shake my head like he's a traitor. I wonder, if he and EEOC weren't here, would the boss be telling nigger jokes too. The boss continues with the jokes and the room is getting stuffy. I tell DeMarcus I'm going out to get Danny to check the thermostat. It's hot as fucking hell in here, I say. The har-har-haring is so loud I don't even have to whisper.

When I come back I'm moving around the table, setting out steak knives and crumbing, and when I get to the boss he puts his hand on my elbow and says affably, We're not offending you with any of this, are we? Ha! I say to the boss. You think I haven't heard this before? I give him a matronly smile with this but he's already patting my elbow and turning away.

The air conditioner must have gone out again. It's a chronic problem in this room, and I notice that jackets are off and collars unbuttoned. EEOC is the only one who doesn't seem to notice the heat, or else he's deliberately resistant to shedding any layers around these guys. The building is really old, it was built in the forties, and though the owner is a millionaire he's notoriously cheap. It might cost $15,000 to replace the A/C but he won't do it. He made his money in the seventies by investing in the development of the first heart stent. He keeps demand up, feeding all these people meat slathered in butter.

I corner Danny in the bar. Danny, you got to do something about the A/C, I plead, I really don't need to see these guys take off any more clothing. Danny says All right all right sista I'm on it and I know that means *I don't give a fuck if they get heatstroke and die in there*. At least I've made the gesture of looking out for them, at least if one of them bitches to him on the way out about how hot it was it won't be news to Danny and I'm covered. He'll be ready to say *I know brother I know, we had our man working on it all night, I can't fucking believe it went out while you got all your guys here, you of all people, I know it was a big night for you, how was everything else?* But when I get back in the room I think maybe the heat has sobered them up some because in the din I hear the boss say But I can't tell this one in mixed company. They've killed our last four cases of the

'99 vintage and we've had to move on to the 2000, so when he says this I'm facing into the corner of the room, opening another bottle. I roll my eyes, looking down at the landscape on the Joseph Phelps label, but I don't leave and I hear him mutter something about he'll tell it later so I go ahead and pour around the table and take a coffee order. I say Would you care for cognac or espresso with dessert? I never say cappuccino or latte even though we can do it.

I learned that from Nic Martinez, in this room. I was assigned to be his bitch and he resented having to split the take with me because it was a preset and he could have done it on his own. I didn't fuck up anything on the first three courses but at the end he heard me say coffee cappuccino and he pinched the back of my elbow hard. In the corner of the room he said Do you want him to like you? nodding at our busser. I didn't know what to say so I said What do you mean? It's not a trick question, he said. You put him in the mother foaming milk for twenty minutes he's gonna hate you, and I am too. And don't say coffee it's free on a preset. I thought he was off me forever because of that but later the same week I walked past the Private and he asked me if I partied. I didn't know what he meant then either but I said yes and that was the beginning of something. He was resetting the table with his partner just like he'd done with me. I went home with him that night and he made me some microwaved apple-cinnamon oatmeal and told me he loved my big juicy ass. In his bed when he said Are you gonna get it I lied and said yes and when he asked me if I got it I lied again.

The Private Room is where Lou Ambrogetti bent me over in the dark, over there where the wine bucket is now.

The room where the expo Estéban kissed me one night, walked up to me with all kinds of purpose and kissed me. I kissed him back for no reason.

————

They're all finishing their desserts so we're clearing the last of the plates but they're still drinking hard. Lushie is on his seventh or eighth whiskey and he's guzzling the wine too. The goal seems to be not so much pleasure as obliteration. Somebody puts his arm around my waist, a liberty taken with me fairly often because I'm small and just the right height. You sign up for a certain kind of life and shell out the dough for it, you expect the waitresses to permit you. I turn toward the guy to see what he wants. He's so drunk he's beaming but he's been here before, he keeps his words standing up as he asks, Sunshine, can we smoke our cigars in here?

No sir, I say, I'm sorry, there's no smoking in the building, it's a city ordinance. I tug away from his arm and notice that one of the others seems to be asking DeMarcus the same question at the other end of the table, he's gesturing with his cigar and when DeMarcus shakes his head he looks just as disappointed as the one who called me Sunshine. That guy sticks his cigar in his mouth anyway and starts chewing on it.

Everything is winding down and DeMarcus says he's going to go put the check together, which can take a while on these parties. I say I'll stay in the room to watch over them till he gets back but I feel like I need to get out for a minute and everybody's topped off except Lushie. I can't keep up with him and I'm not worrying about it any longer, so I step into the hall and lean against the wall in the dark space between two stacks of chairs.

Benito, one of the bussers, comes around the corner into the hall and pulls a stack of the chairs away from the wall. When he sees me he jumps a little and says ¡Maestra! ¡Me has asustado!

Sorry, Papi, I say. Benito is probably close to sixty but quite spry and often he'll help me out on my tables even when he hasn't been assigned to my station. I'll be holding a stack of cleared plates away from my body, leaning down over a table to answer someone's question, and suddenly I'll feel the weight of the plates being lifted from me. By the time I can turn to look he'll already be halfway to the dishroom. One of his sons, also named Benito though we call him Sanchez, is the barback; another, Orlando called Magic, works the salad line; and his youngest, whose given name I don't know because everyone calls him Niño, is also a busser. The sons all have their father's work ethic and Danny will joke with Benito that he needs to bring his other sons over too. Papi, you got any more where these came from? he'll say. Benito does, actually, and he'll say Sí, jefe, sí.

Good peoples? he asks me, with a nod toward the wall behind me, referring to my party on the other side of it. This question is strictly economic—it never means Do you like them? It means only Are they spending money?

Sí, Papi, I say, muchísimo vino.

Es bueno, es bueno, he clucks as he disappears around the corner with the chairs.

When I open the door this time I step into a thick quiet, the sleepy quiet of the overstuffed and oversoused. If they were younger they'd be boisterous and obnoxious, they'd be cranking up at this point, but those days are behind them and many of them seem calmed by the cigars they're holding in their teeth. The boss is standing up at the end of the table opposite me, and at my entrance he pauses in the middle of another joke. He looks at me and says Hi. Everyone else turns to look at me. I'm surprised at this late acknowledgment and I say hi back and stand still. In this job you learn to give them what they want and not take anything personally but I've got Asami's frisky defiant burr up in my skin and I say You're gonna stop now? This is the one I *want* to hear!

No one laughs at my joke. I'm like Lushie earlier, talking about aortal aneurisms. I turn around to get the hell out and I nearly knock down DeMarcus with the door. Whoa, he says, what got into you?

————

I am sitting on an upturned glass rack, vigorously working the spots off spoons still hot from the washer, when DeMarcus comes to tell me they're leaving. Cal thinks it's bad form to let your guests leave without telling them good night and if he caught me sitting here doing my sidework instead of seeing them off he'd call me out. *Just gonna let your people walk out like that, huh? How much money did that spoon pay you tonight? Make sure you give that spoon your card: Hey, Spoon, ask for me next time you bring in Knife and Fork, I'll take great care of you. DeMarcus, remind me not to have dinner at Marie's house, she one of those Don't let the door hit you on the way out hosts. Classy.*

I leave the silverware half-finished and walk with DeMar-

cus back to The Private Room. We stand in the doorway
while the men file out, shaking their hands like two pastors
after a church service. Thank you, gentlemen. Thank you
so much, sir. Thanks for coming in tonight. Appreciate your
business. Congratulations, hope you enjoyed everything.
How'd we do tonight? Everybody happy?

———

After we get out DeMarcus and I hang in the employee
parking lot, waiting for Asami, who promised to share some
of her stash with us. We have half a bottle of the party's
cab and a full bottle of the chardonnay they left in the ice
bucket untouched, and we drink both of them, pouring tall
into Styrofoam cups, one white and one red, sharing. I make
sure to leave a glass in the chard bottle in case Asami wants
some. Other servers and bussers shoot out the back door like
pinballs, letting the door crash against the side of the building and stripping off pieces of their uniform as they head
toward their cars, calling Good night and other more exul-
tant things like Home fucking free! to us as they leave.

Niño must have been the first busser out, because he's
driving back into the parking lot from a beer run—whichever
of the cooks or bussers gets out first takes his turn to buy a
case of Modelo Especial or Bud Light before the stores stop
selling at midnight. He lets down the tailgate of his pickup
and offers DeMarcus and me a beer. There's something about
the way Niño's navy work shirt is always starched stiff, and
something about the way his hair is always trim and gelled,
and something about the way he makes eye contact with you
when he's taking plates from you as if to say, *Give me all*

that. I'll take care of it for you, no problem. Sometimes he actually says things just like this. If you're female he might say *I got it, baby,* but you never feel condescended to, only happy he's in league with you.

He's so young, only nineteen, but his wife had twins in San Luis Potosí. He got the call after work one night a couple months ago, standing about where he is now. He was overjoyed, he started to cry, and everyone started hugging him and saying Congratulations Papa! and ¡Felicidades! and we all went over to the bar next door and bought him and everyone else in the place a shot of Patrón. He talks about how he's saving all his money to bring them over so they can be raised in America, he tells me he gave each of them one English and one Spanish name: Thomas José and Michael Alonzo.

I tip him more than I tip the other bussers, because he works so hard and I like his attitude. It pays to hustle, it pays to bend over, we both know this. You keep your standards high and your work strong but these are necessary for success; you keep your dignity separate, somewhere else, attached to different things.

When Asami finally comes out the back door I say Hey Sandra, how you living?

Dirty, fucking dirty, she says. I pop a Modelo and hold it out to her. Here, honey, just wash it all away, I say.

Thanks, but I think some of it's gonna stick, she says.

Nah, says DeMarcus. Only if you let it.

That right, De? I ask. He shrugs, then says to Niño, What do you think, Francisco?

When DeMarcus says his name, which I repeat in my

head several times for safekeeping, Niño suddenly seems older to me, but he doesn't have any more wisdom on the matter than the rest of us. All he says is, No sé, Marco. Es mi job, ¿sabes?

————

DeMarcus has fantastic teeth and tight waves. He's tall and lanky and he smells good. He keeps taking care of me in the parking lot, passing me the green hit when Asami refreshes the bowl, lighting my cigarettes, opening beers for me. The two of us are having a good time—it's easier on the nights you make money. On the low-scoring nights you feel depressed as hell even if you tell yourself that's the way it is, inconsistent. You can't look at the money on the night, you have to wait for the week or even the month to look at it, and you can't start going home when they overschedule. You have to work it like a nine-to-five even though it's anything but. Asami is hustling hard-core right now, she's the speech teacher at an inner-city public high school in Fort Worth but three nights a week she drives over here too. She can't stay out late like she used to. In the old times we'd wake up together at somebody's apartment and she'd give me a ride back to my car at the restaurant, the day looking gray as an old sock through our hangovers. I offer her the last of the chard but she says she has to go now or she'll be hurting too bad tomorrow.

You can tell she really loves her kids at the school and that's the job she takes seriously. Not that you can blow this one off—turnover at The Restaurant is ridiculous because new people don't realize quick enough they're in the army now and they'd better step up, Chef isn't kidding when he expects you to know all fifteen ingredients in the hoisin sauce that goes with the fried lobster. I've hung in long enough now that they've asked me to sub for a manager on occasion, wear a sexy little dress suit and heels and help out when we're short-staffed. So far I've said no. I know they see you in the suit and you do a good job and before you know it that's where they want you all the time, and then everybody else's fuckups are on you instead of just your own. Plus I'd never see my kid if I started managing and I hardly see her anyway. All right, I'm out, love you guys see you Thursday, Asami says, putting her bowl back where it lives in the glovebox of her car. Peace, Mama, says DeMarcus, and I tell her to be careful driving all that way home. Niño and the cooks and bussers have cleared out so when she's gone it's just me and De, we get into my car and he cranks up my Erykah. *Push up the fader / Bust the meter / Shake the tweeter / Bump it* he sings along, grooving in his seat. I saw her in Whole Foods the other day, he says, damn, woman is a *woman*. Talk to her? I ask. Naw, he says, I'm gonna say Excuse me Miss Badu, got me a fine position of employment as a servant, can I take you out sometime? Whole Foods guy probably has a better shot than me.

Whole Foods guy didn't make three bucks tonight like you did, I say. Hey, partna, it was smooth, smooth tonight, he says, offering his fist for a bump. I work with you whenever you want, anytime, he adds. Likewise, baby, I say, and then, I wish Asami had left us some. There's a long high pause while we listen to Erykah rock it and I feel him thinking something through. Got some at the house, he says finally. Is that an invitation? I ask. It is if you want it to be, he says.

His brother drops him off at The Restaurant and picks him up when's it over, and when J—I've never heard DeMarcus call him anything else—pulls into the parking lot I'm drunk and stoned and I have no idea where they live or how I will get back to my car but I get into the cab of the truck between them on the bench seat. It's an old green Ford, from before they started making everything on cars so round. It smells like smoke. J has the hip-hop station pounding and looks at me like he knew this would happen, his face still, absent. He nods, doesn't speak. I can tell he's on something that's taken him up so far he can see me from above. Crack? I tried crack only once and it didn't work and now I'm hoping I have some limits. He drives out of the parking lot and I feel DeMarcus relax next to me, he's realizing I'm committed, realizing I'm down. He puts his hand on my thigh and then we're making out, the cab of this truck is old-school huge and I swing myself into his lap, facing him, feeling him hard as glass through my thin dress pants. J turns up the music as he pulls onto the freeway. I am grinding on DeMarcus and it's not enough, I feel like my body will do this without me if it has to. I feel nothing but his hands on my hips and his lips all over my collarbone and the 808 kicking out of the stereo, a primal rhythm I can't resist any more than the blood pulsing in my cunt. She want it, observes J, looking over at us. He has gold teeth. Not solid gold, the kind with the gold edges.

DeMarcus unbuckles his belt and starts undoing his

pants, it's like he has four hands because he's getting his
pants down and turning me to face J at the same time, pushing me gently onto my knees in the middle of the seat, he's
behind me reaching around me to pull off my pants too. He
can't find the button and I've got one hand on J's thigh and
one hand on the headrest behind him, I'm concentrating
on reminding my drunk self to not grab the steering wheel
to hold steady. My pants are too big, I've lost weight from
doing blow after work. DeMarcus can't wait so he just pulls
them down, they catch briefly on my hips but he tugs and
then he's pushing inside me and I'm pushing back. J I'm in it,
he shouts over the music and I watch J's face, he doesn't look
at me right next to him, keeps his eyes on the road and says
Tight? I feel DeMarcus slow down so he won't come and he
says Shit fuck sweet pussy. Then he asks me do I want to get
J in on it and I don't say anything I just take the hand that is
on J's thigh and I rub his cock through his track pants. He
still doesn't look at me. Suck on me, he says. I bend down and
DeMarcus backs up, still inside me, until his back is against
the door so I have room to be like a stretching cat between
them. I suck on J long and right and he starts breathing deep
and making sounds and he takes one hand off the steering
wheel and puts it in my hair, puts it on my head, I can tell
he wants to push on my head. I go faster hoping he won't
and then DeMarcus starts moving again. I count when I give
head or I repeat something over and over in my mind, one-
syllable strokes. *Sex. Is. The. Same. But. The. Dishes.* I say
to his cock. This is mean head I'm giving now. It's firm and
I'm not letting it be wet but this J won't even look at me so.
There was a man once to whose penis I said *I. Love. You.*

So. Much. I. Would. Do. Any. thing. For. You. Can. You. Tell. and every time I got to that *Tell* I would moan Mmm and he would say Oh my God, what are you doing to me but this is not that man. This is me in a truck on Highway 183, this is me drunk and high, this is me doing and being done. J says, I wanna switch and I feel the truck slowing down. He stops the truck on the shoulder of the freeway and rams the gearshift up the column to park. I barely have time to get my mouth off him before he's out of the cab and then there's a damp thwack as DeMarcus pulls out of me abruptly, he opens the passenger door and crosses in front of the truck, trotting, he doesn't button his pants just lets his long work shirt hang over everything. His brother is in the cab next to me pulling my hips down on top of his cock before DeMarcus has even gotten into the driver's seat.

DeMarcus glides the truck along the shoulder until he can get back on the freeway and without being told I take his cock into my mouth, tasting myself. *I. Am. An. An. i. mal. Good. Then. You. Fire. Her.* I think about my daughter, how her eyelids turn lavender at night. I think about how my friend Hal, who also works at The Restaurant and also has a daughter, told me I should never do anything I wouldn't want her to do. How one afternoon he said to me You know Rie, we're doing what we want. If we wanted to be with them we would. We have to face that and decide what's next. If I wanted to be with Blair I would move to Houston and work at Starbucks if I had to. It's just money. *She. Had. Twins. Mine. Died.*

J is hardly moving back there behind me, although he's as stiff as his brother. I feel DeMarcus turn to look at him and I wonder what he sees to make him say J? J, you with us? Then I feel J drop down to the seat from where he'd been up on his knees against me, he moves so fast his cock goes sideways as it comes out of me and it hurts. I stop sucking on DeMarcus to turn and look at J, who's leaning against the passenger-side window. I think he may have passed out. Girl, you don't have to stop, says DeMarcus, so I put my mouth back on his cock and give him the good head with my hand and the wetness until he says Ahhh, shit! Oh shit, girl! Don't stop, don't stop, and then he lets it all go. There's nowhere for me to spit it and I don't feel like swallowing. If I don't swallow while I'm taking it, if I hesitate, then I never want to. I have an undershirt on so I pull my work shirt over my head. I wad it up under my mouth like a big handkerchief and soundlessly push the semen out of my mouth and into the shirt, careful not to spill any. The shirt already has steak sauce, wine, butter, and sweat on it. Roll down your window, I tell DeMarcus, and when he does I lean across him and look behind us to make sure it's not going to catch on somebody's windshield or antenna and then I let it fly. So the stories are true, smiles DeMarcus. You off the chain, girl.

After five days of driving we stop in front of their house, which is small. The porch light is on and I see vinyl siding, a tricycle on the sidewalk. DeMarcus and I get out of the truck and walk toward the house, leaving J in the cab. Where are we and whose is that, I ask, pointing at the tricycle. Shh, he says, opening the door. In the front room an old man is sitting in an easy chair holding a can of Budweiser and watching television. Hey Pop, says DeMarcus. Where J? says the old man. Sleep in the truck, answers DeMarcus, I be back with him shortly, how you? The old man grunts in response, he never looks away from the television or acknowledges me.

Want to shower? DeMarcus asks me. I say How much? and he looks at me like he doesn't get it. When he said Want to shower? I thought *He wants to put me somewhere where I can't see what's about to happen with J* and I thought *I want to shower so much* and I thought *Some of it's gonna stick* and I thought *How can I ever get back from here* and what came out was How much?

Do I smell like fries? I ask, trying to act like I am keeping it together, trying to pretend I didn't just say something incomprehensible. The Restaurant is Zagat-rated and our party spent over four grand on one dinner that involved compotes, reductions, infusions, compound butters, a coulis, a pan jus, but somehow the smell of French fries is what I always carry home on me. He puts his nose in my neck and inhales tenderly. We're still standing right there in the living room in front of his dad. Crème brûlée, he says. Come on, I'll show you to the ladies'.

This is the thing about the service industry, you can get trained to be slick and hospitable in any situation and it serves you well the rest of your life. Once you figure out that everything is performance and you bow to that, learn to modulate, you can dissociate from the mothership of yourself like an astronaut floating in space. That's how you can show a fucked-in-your-truck girl down the hall to the ladies' and tell her her neck smells like crème brûlée in front of a zombie dad while some freebased flesh you're related to waits for you to carry it inside. That's how the crunked girl can get in the shower like she's told and stand over the drain and pee and not think about what might happen next.

———

I lose track of time in the shower. I wash my vagina and then stand there letting the water run over me. I'm hearing the water like it's a waterfall, loud and like I'm inside it, when I'm high I hear sixteen layers of sound. I hear someone come into the bathroom, hear a belt buckle hit the floor. DeMarcus pulls back the shower curtain and steps in behind me. Clean yet? he asks. How's your brother? I ask. He be all right, just gets carried away with the shit sometimes. Whose tricycle is that outside? I ask again. Excuse me, he says, stepping around me to get near the water, turning his back to me. My son's, he says finally. How did I not know you have a son? I ask. He turns around but his hands are over his face, he's rubbing his eyes. He shrugs. Work is work, he says. Don't everybody got to know everything.

We get out of the shower and cross the hall into a bedroom. It's dark, the shades are drawn, there is a bed shoved against the wall and J is lying on it, his back to the wall. His eyes are closed. Porn is playing on a television at the foot of the bed. DeMarcus is wearing a towel around his waist and disappears into the darkest corner of the room until he strikes a match and I see that he's lighting a cigar. He candles the end and then turns it and puffs three times until it's lit. He sits down on the edge of the bed and pats the place beside him. I sit down, I am naked and cold. I stare at the television but I hate porn. De is watching it and his eyes are bloodshot.

He says Let's lie down so we do, he is on the outer edge of the bed with his ankles crossed and I am between him and J, who is silent and still. I have my head on De's chest and I doze off lying on him while he smokes his cigar and watches a jarhead fuck a stripper on stage. She has her hair in two ponytails and he holds on to them like handles.

———

I wake up when I feel myself drooling on his chest. I wipe his chest and then my mouth. Sorry, I say. Happens, he says, no problem. You ready to go back? I'll drive you. Sure, I say, thanks. I notice that J is gone but I don't ask where he went. I feel something feathery on my skin. I get off the bed and can see by the bruised dawn light coming around the window shade that the bed is covered in cigar ash. Covered. Evenly, as if it is some new weather. His dad is not in the chair when we leave.

In the truck on the way back we don't say much. My head hurts. I see a sign that tells me we are in Irving. Working tonight? I ask DeMarcus. I'm off, he says, you? I say I am and he says You never take off do you and I say I don't. We're quiet until we get near the restaurant and he says If you want that morning-after pill I'll pay you back for it.

I hadn't thought of that. Do I need it? I ask, more to myself than him. Couldn't hurt, he says. Yeah, all right, I'll let you know, I say. I don't tell him I already have a dose at home because the last time they gave me an extra. It was fifty bucks and I don't mind letting him pay it backward for me so I'll tell him how much it cost next time I see him.

As he drives away I get in my car and I think *We never*

even smoked the weed he said he had at the house and then I stare at the back of the restaurant and wish there were more hours between now and seeing it again later today. It's seven in the morning and I have to be here at five this evening. I drive home, home to my clean apartment, to my clean bed. I take another shower and I take the first Plan B pill and I take some ibuprofen and I call my daughter's father because it's rare that I'm awake this early, when he's getting her ready for school. I ask if I can talk to her and then I hear her high-pitched voice say Hi Mama and I hear her crunching toast. I ask her what kind of jelly she's having today. I tell her I miss her. She asks if she can come up to the restaurant like last time, for a Shirley Temple. I say We'll see. I imagine Hal in the green apron, smiling and asking What can I get started for you? He is thirty-four and has braces.

I go to sleep at eight and wake up at three. Her school day. I make coffee and wonder if I have any diseases now. We have been warned there might be a test on the hand-sell wines this week so I review them. *'01 Stags' Leap Winery, Napa, $90 down from $120. Ruby red, plum, earth, green tea, velvety tannins, complex.* Wine is all words. People who know wine don't need your help and people who don't will believe anything you say if it sounds good. Our sommelier would think that was a shitty attitude to have.

I eat a piece of vegetarian sausage while I stand in the kitchen drinking my perfect coffee and reading over the hand-sells. I look lean and I wear a digital sport watch on my left wrist so sometimes my guests will ask me if I run. I don't say No I'm just snorting a lot of coke right now. I say that I do run and they say I bet you don't eat much meat do you and I say No actually I'm vegetarian and they laugh at this because I have just shown them a tray of ten pounds of raw beef carved into the different cuts of steak we offer. I hype it, the tiny mystique of my being vegetarian and working there. I say Meat is my profession, which often leads someone at the table to say Well you're certainly a professional. I don't say *I know, because I've made a hundred people before you say that same thing in this same situation, I've made you remember your charming professional vegetarian server when it's time for you to put a number on the tip line,* and I don't say, *I'm not vegetarian because of the animals, I'm vegetarian because I hate the way meat feels in my mouth.*

At four I get in the shower, scrubbing everything hard. I pluck my eyebrows, brush my teeth, do my makeup, fix my hair, file and buff my nails. They see your hands more than anything. I put on my pants and undershirt and grab all my tools. I put the second Plan B pill in my pocket and hope I will remember to take it when everything is madness at eight o'clock. I stop at the cleaner's to swap soiled for pressed, I have a good man on the corner of Greenville and Belmont who does my shirts the way I want them and doesn't charge much. He starches everything to spec, so my long bistro apron can stand on its own and the creases in my sleeves will be so pointy that even at ten thirty tonight when I walk up to my last table for the first time they will see those creases and they'll trust me just a little. My name is Marie, and I'll take care of you tonight.

Acknowledgments

This book owes most of its existence to Ben Fountain, who was the first person to champion and publish my writing, and whose friendship and encouragement have never wavered. He is the most generous writer I know, and I am grateful to have had the guidance of his example.

For telling me my restaurant stories were a book before I knew it myself, and for feeding me in Iowa City better than I'll ever be fed again, Xander Maksik. I aspire to hone my aesthetics, in life and in art, to the razor's edge where Xander lives. It's hard to know someone who exists and writes with the purpose and ferocity of a bullet and not feel intimidated, but it's very good for quashing internal excuses. Also for forcing me to have fun, for sharing the whole ride of "emerging" with me, and for freakishly good advice on all fronts.

To Gregory Sherl, Roxane Gay, ZZ Packer, Kathy Pories, David Hale Smith, Erica Mena Landry, Lee Fountain, Willard Spiegelman, and the editorial staffs of *CutBank* and

Reunion: The Dallas Review for loving, selecting, publishing, and/or nominating my stories.

To my teachers Ethan Canin, for crushing my fear of structure and for appreciating what I do well, and Michael Martone, for infectious excitement.

To Jon and Leslie Maksik, for the beauty and peace of Sun Valley and for hospitality of the highest form.

To the Iowa Writers' Workshop, the Rona Jaffe Foundation Writers' Awards, and the National Book Foundation, for invaluable financial and psychological support.

To my agent, Anna Stein O'Sullivan, and my editor, Coralie Hunter, for making my book better and this first trip good.

To Charlie Drum, for stepping in as a miraculous surrogate grandparent and showing my children the time of their lives in Iowa City and beyond. Knowing your kids are with someone who loves them as much as you do while you try to write opens up impressive stores of energy and focus.

To my mom, for the books, and my dad, for how to tell a story.

For everything, Chad Wilhite.

And for seeing me, wanting me, knowing me, trusting me, making me laugh enough to dispel two decades of sadness, loving me right, and letting me be deeply happy for the first time in my life, Evan Stone.